DEAR SISTER

Jessica looked down at her sister Elizabeth's figure, frozen on the hospital bed in pale, unmoving silence.

"Liz, can you hear me? Please, Lizzie. It was my fault you got hurt. Lizzie, I can't go through the rest of my life without you! You have got to get well. I need you so much!"

Elizabeth remained motionless. Jessica's eyes filled with tears that quickly rolled down her cheeks.

She took her twin's limp hand in hers and pleaded, "You know how much I love you, how much everybody loves you. Lizzie, oh, Lizzie, please hear me! You just can't die!"

Elizabeth's hand remained slack. There was no answering squeeze, no flickering of eyelids. There was absolutely nothing.

Bantam Books in the Sweet Valley High Series
Ask your bookseller for the books you have missed

SWEET VALLEY HIGH

DEAR SISTER

Written by
Kate William

Created by
FRANCINE PASCAL

BANTAM BOOKS
TORONTO • NEW YORK • LONDON • SYDNEY • AUCKLAND

RL6, IL age 12 and up

DEAR SISTER
A Bantam Book / April 1984

Sweet Valley High is a trademark of Francine Pascal

Conceived by Francine Pascal
Produced by Cloverdale Press, Inc.

Cover art by James Mathewuse

ISBN 0-553-26622-5

Published simultaneously in the United States and Canada

Bantam Books are published by Bantam Books, Inc. Its trademark, consisting of
the words "Bantam Books" and the portrayal of a rooster, is Registered in
U.S. Patent and Trademark Office and in other countries. Marca Registrada.
Bantam Books, Inc., 666 Fifth Avenue, New York, New York 10103.

PRINTED IN THE UNITED STATES OF AMERICA

O   20   19   18   17   16   15   14

To Alexandra Guarnaschelli

One

Elizabeth Wakefield lay still on the high, narrow hospital bed—as still as if she were dead, her twin sister Jessica thought. As she stood looking down at the motionless body, tears rolled down Jessica's cheeks. Day after day she had sat beside her sister's bed in Joshua Fowler Memorial Hospital waiting for her to regain consciousness.

"Lizzie, oh, Lizzie, please hear me," Jessica sobbed. "You can't die!"

Although Elizabeth and Jessica were identical twins, it was far from obvious now. Before the terrible motorcycle accident that had put Elizabeth in a coma, it was extremely difficult to tell the beautiful sixteen-year-old girls apart. When people in the sunny town of Sweet Valley, California, saw a five-foot-six gloriously attrac-

1

tive young girl with sun-streaked blond hair and sparkling blue-green eyes, they knew it was *one* of the Wakefield twins, but they couldn't always be sure which one.

Now the difference was striking, and heartbreaking to see. Elizabeth, once vibrant and lively, was frozen in pale, unmoving silence. She hardly resembled the vivacious girl she had been just a few days earlier. Jessica's fresh, youthful beauty was still very much in evidence, but it was marred by a worried expression, eyes red from crying, and a frown of pain and sorrow that seemed to have become permanent.

Jessica's fixed expression of misery had been there since her sister was brought into the emergency room after the motorcycle accident. Jessica had ridden in the ambulance with Elizabeth. Their parents, Ned and Alice Wakefield, had raced to the hospital, as had the twins' older brother Steven. They had all seen that stricken look on Jessica's face and assured her Elizabeth would be all right. But as the days went by and Elizabeth remained silent, Jessica's fears grew and the look of misery deepened.

Now, she sat down slowly on the chair next to her sister's bed. Looking at the medical equipment, she shivered. She knew the IV going into Elizabeth's arm fed her sister life-sustaining nutrients. But the other tubes and machines frightened her.

Jessica took Elizabeth's limp hand in hers and pleaded, "Lizzie, you know how much I love you, how much everybody loves you. They love you more than me! You just can't die, Lizzie. I can't go through the rest of my life without you."

Elizabeth's hand remained slack. There was no answering squeeze, no flickering of eyelids. There was absolutely nothing.

A hand fell on Jessica's shoulder. Startled, she jerked her head up. Her blue-green eyes met a pair of soft brown ones in a kind face.

"Miss Wakefield?"

"Yes."

"I could see the resemblance. You're both beautiful."

Jessica regarded the man in his white lab coat, afraid of the news he might bring.

"I can only guess how painful it is for you to see your sister like this."

"I'm so worried!"

The man stooped so that his face was on a level with hers.

"Jessica, we're doing everything we can for Elizabeth. We're trying our best to make her well. Do you understand what I'm saying?"

She nodded mutely. Did he mean Elizabeth was going to be OK, or . . .

"My name is John Edwards. I'm the neuro-surgeon on your sister's case."

"Dr. Edwards?"

"That's right, Jessica. Your sister is in a coma. You know what that is, don't you?"

"It means Liz is going to die!" Jessica's voice cracked, and the tears started again. She sobbed as if her heart were breaking.

She felt strong hands on her shoulders, shaking her gently but insistently. "Stop it, Jessica. Crying isn't going to help your sister. Elizabeth needs your strength, not your tears."

Jessica raised a tearstained face. "You don't understand!"

"I know how upset you are."

"You don't understand, Dr. Edwards," she said again. "It's my fault, all my fault."

"Jessica, were you driving the car that hit the motorcycle?"

"No, of course not!"

"Then why is it your fault?" he asked kindly.

"Because I was supposed to give her a ride! I was selfish and left without her so she had to go with Todd on his motorcycle. If I'd waited, she wouldn't. . . . Oh, I should have waited. It *is* my fault!"

Suddenly Dr. Edwards's hands were cupping her face, forcing her to look up. "Jessica, accidents happen. They aren't anyone's fault. And right now, blame isn't important. Guiding Elizabeth back to all of us is. That's what we have to do. You and your brother and your parents have to bring Elizabeth back. I'll help, Jessica, but it's really up to you."

"Me?"

"Yes. You're the person closest to her. *You* have the best chance of reaching her."

"How? How do I reach her?"

"Talk to her. Just talk to her." He ran his fingers through his dark brown hair, walked to the window, and stared blankly. Suddenly he turned, and Jessica saw anger and frustration in his face.

"Jessica, doctors can keep people alive with machines, but we can't will them to come back to us. Sometimes, it doesn't happen, no matter how much you or I want it. The only thing we can do is try."

"I'll try. I'll do anything for Liz."

"I know you will. Take care of your sister, and I'll be in later to check on her."

As soon as the doctor was gone, Jessica looked down at Elizabeth's quiet figure.

"Liz, can you hear me? Please, Lizzie. It was my fault you got hurt. Well, maybe not *all* my fault, but I know you would never have let me down like that. I don't know how you do it. When you tell someone you're going to be somewhere, you're there. People can count on you. Only a jerk would count on me. Lizzie, I promise to be more responsible in the future. But I can't do it without you.

You have to get well, Liz! I need you so much!"

The figure on the bed remained motionless.

"Jess, why don't we go down to the cafeteria for a cup of tea?"

Jessica jumped. Right now, the world consisted only of her sister and herself. She'd been so involved she hadn't even heard her mother come into the room.

"Oh, Mom, I'm so scared!" she sobbed, tears streaming down her cheeks.

"Jess, honey, don't cry like this. Elizabeth isn't going to die. We won't let her! You'll see, darling. She'll come out of this, and everything will be the same as it was before the accident."

Jessica wanted to believe her mother's words. She wished with all her heart that she could turn back the clock to the night Elizabeth had been hurt.

Normally, Elizabeth would have gone to Enid Rollins's sweet-sixteen party with her boyfriend Todd Wilkins, but Todd had had to be at a party for his grandfather early in the evening. Since he'd promised to get away as soon as possible and join Elizabeth at the country club, she hadn't minded too much arriving at the party with Jessica and her date for the night, Brian. She hadn't even been upset when Todd called midway through the party to tell her he would be later than he'd expected. But she'd been furious when he hadn't shown up until the party was over.

Still, Elizabeth loved Todd so much that even a broken date couldn't keep her mad at him for long, especially when she found out where he'd been. Todd had been making a deal to sell his motorcycle. Elizabeth couldn't believe it when he told her. Owning that bike had been a dream of Todd's ever since he was a little kid. But he was selling it now because it was making problems between Elizabeth and him, and because he loved her.

Elizabeth had looked over at the bike. Suddenly she wasn't afraid of it anymore, or of what her parents would do if they ever found out she'd taken a ride on it. She thought about it for a moment. Since Jessica had left without her, she had no way of getting to the Caravan, the club where the rest of the kids had gone after Enid's party. She was stranded. Unless . . .

Then she made the decision, perhaps the worst one of her life. She got on the bike.

At first, nothing could have felt better than to ride behind the boy she loved as the motorcycle leaned into the curves of the road, the wind whipping through her hair. And she hadn't even seen the out-of-control van coming toward them until it was too late.

* * *

"Liz, answer me, please!" Jessica urged from her sister's bedside. "How about if I say it was all my fault? Would that bring you back? I'll make a deal with you, Lizzie. I'll take all the blame, and you'll live. What do you say?"

Desperation warred with hopelessness in Jessica's mind. "It's not fair," she cried. "Crunch McAllister wasn't even hurt when he hit Todd's bike with his van, and Todd wasn't, either. But you're in a coma, and you never did a single thing to deserve it. Oh, Liz, I want everything to be like it was before. I want to tease you about your writing. You never got mad at me for that, did you? You always understand me, Liz. Nobody else does, not even me sometimes. I guess that's the big difference between us. You can get into other people's heads and then do things that make them feel better." Jessica sat quietly for a few minutes, feeling helpless.

"Darn it, Liz, wake up! You absolutely cannot do this to me. You know very well I can't cope without you. You're being selfish—and I'll never forgive you if you die!"

Just when she thought she was totally out of tears, they came again. "Oh, no! I must be a beast to talk like this to you, Liz!"

"Jessica?"

She whirled around to find Dr. Edwards looking at her with concern.

"Jessica, when I told you to talk to Elizabeth, I had something else in mind."

"I did something wrong?"

"Not wrong, but not what I had in mind."

"What should I do?"

"I've got an idea, Jessica." He grinned at her reassuringly, ruffling her sun-streaked hair. "Just talk to your sister about everyday things. Don't lay your guilt on her. Talk about family, school, boys—whatever. Just chat, as if you expected her to understand and answer."

"That will bring her out of it?"

"No promises, Jessica. Maybe yes, maybe no. Isn't it worth a try?"

"I'll try anything if it will help Liz."

So, for the next two days, Elizabeth's twilight world was bombarded with memories.

"Remember the time I tried to take Todd away from you? I would have killed someone for doing that to me, but not you. You were willing to step aside if I was the one Todd really liked. But *you* were always the one he wanted, Liz. And he was right to pick you. No wonder everyone loves you. You're good and kind, and you really care about other people. Take Enid Rollins, for example. She's world-class dull, for heaven's sake. But she's your friend so you always stick up for her. When I blabbed her secret to everybody, you were right there defending her. Now I'm sorry for the way I acted, Liz, and

I promise I'll never make another crack about Enid, ever!

"Do you mind if I say something about your makeup, Liz? Don't get me wrong, you always look *good*, but with more eye makeup and blusher, you could be sensational. And your clothes. Jeans and button-down shirts are OK, but sometimes you're too conservative. When you get out of here, we've got to go shopping. I'll help you pick out some really spectacular outfits, OK?

"You are going to get well, Liz, I just know it. You're going to get back into things at school. You're still the star reporter of *The Oracle*. No one else could write the "Eyes and Ears" column as well as you do. You always manage to keep it light and funny. You know, Liz, I bet it's probably the only gossip column in the world people actually *want* to be in. You never make anyone look bad. And I'm sorry, Liz, I really am sorry for trying to talk you into putting items in about me just because I'm your sister. I swear I'll never do that again.

"Oh, Lizzie," she whispered, "wake up, please. If you'll just wake up, I'll do anything you want me to. I'll be your slave for life!"

Jessica rested her head on the bed, exhausted. She heard a sound and looked up, but she was still alone in the room with Elizabeth. The sound

10

came again, and she turned, trying to figure out where it had come from.

A soft moan came from the still figure on the bed.

"Liz?"

Jessica burst out into the corridor.

"Mom! Dad! Dr. Edwards! Somebody! She's awake!"

In seconds a small crowd had gathered in Elizabeth's room. Alice and Ned Wakefield were so nervous they could hardly breathe as Dr. Edwards examined Elizabeth.

He straightened and turned to them with a smile. "I think your daughter has decided to come back to us!"

"Dr. Edwards, you're the most wonderful person in the world," Jessica cried.

"You deserve a lot of the credit, Jessica."

"I do?" Jessica shivered with pride, relief, and just plain ecstasy. Elizabeth was awake, and she'd helped!

Alice Wakefield bent over the bed. "Liz? Sweetheart, we're here. Can you hear us?"

Eyelids fluttered, but nothing more.

"Doctor?"

"Let Jessica try, Mrs. Wakefield. I think she has a special way of communicating with her sister."

Aware of the eyes on her and glowing with happiness, Jessica walked over to the bed. Everything was going to be wonderful, she just knew it.

"Liz. Hey, Lizzie, time to wake up."

Elizabeth's eyes opened fully. She stared at her twin sister and moistened her dry lips. "Jessica!"

Two

"Hi, Liz, your favorite twin sister is here at last!" Jessica bounced into the hospital room, an overnight bag in one hand, a canvas carryall in the other. She stopped dead in her tracks, however, when she saw Elizabeth crying. Dropping the bags on the floor, she rushed to the bed.

"Liz, what is it? Are you hurting? I'll call a nurse, a doctor!" *Please don't let her have a relapse,* Jessica prayed.

Elizabeth covered her face with her hands and sobbed. "No, don't call anybody. I don't want anybody to see me, Jess!" she cried.

Totally confused, Jessica sank down onto the chair. "What do you mean?"

Elizabeth took her hands away from her face and sat up. "Look at me. Just look at me!"

Jessica stared at her sister, hoping to find a clue for the tears. Elizabeth's face was a little pale, but how could anyone expect to keep a tan lying in a hospital bed? Her blue-green eyes didn't sparkle as brightly as they used to, but time and rest would take care of that. Jessica had to admit that Elizabeth's usually shiny, bouncy blond hair was hanging limply, but none of those things seemed important enough to be upsetting, not after the miracle of coming back to life.

Still mystified, Jessica asked, "Please tell me why you're crying."

"Wouldn't you cry if you looked like me?" Elizabeth shouted the words at her stunned sister.

"*If* I looked like you?" Jessica wished somebody else were there to handle this. "Liz," she said softly, "I *do* look like you. We're twins, remember?"

"Of course I remember," Elizabeth snapped, narrowing her eyes. "What are you trying to tell me, Jess? Are you saying I'm stupid, or maybe crazy because I got hit on the head?"

"For heaven's sake, Liz, I'm not saying you're crazy," Jessica protested. "You've been in an accident—and in a coma until three days ago. You're lucky to be alive."

"And look like this?"

I don't believe this, Jessica thought. Elizabeth

was actually worried about her looks. A part of Jessica thought it strange, but another part was overjoyed. And, of course, she was relieved when she realized her sister's tears didn't mean she was having some sort of relapse. Worrying about looks was something Jessica could easily understand.

"Well, it's a good thing I got here, Lizzie, because this one little bag contains everything you need." Jessica retrieved the canvas carryall and dumped its contents on the bed. "We have got super-duper dry shampoo."

Elizabeth wrinkled her nose. "Dry shampoo?"

"I know it's not as good as the real thing, but it'll help put the life back in your hair. Trust me." Jessica knew she was talking too fast and that her voice was almost too cheerful, but she couldn't seem to stop herself. She didn't want Elizabeth to start crying again.

"I also brought makeup, cologne, lotion—everything. Let's get started on you. We don't have any time to lose because Todd is due here any minute. I knew you'd want to look great for your favorite guy."

"Todd is coming here?" Elizabeth shrank back against the pillows. Having turned away, Jessica missed the look of panic that flitted across her sister's face.

"Isn't that great? The doctors said 'family only,' but I convinced them that a visit from Todd

15

would be therapeutic!" Jessica didn't tell Elizabeth that Todd had managed to sneak in a few times when she was still in a coma. She had a feeling her sister wouldn't have wanted Todd to see her in that condition.

For fifteen minutes Jessica worked on Elizabeth's hair and makeup. Finally she stepped back to check her work before handing Elizabeth a small mirror. "You can thank me now, Liz. Pay me later," Jessica kidded, pleased with the transformation.

Elizabeth stared into the mirror for several moments, then frowned. "I'm still too pale. And my eyes look positively dead," she complained.

"You look great," Jessica protested.

"Let me have that blusher and gloss," Elizabeth ordered. "And the eye makeup, too."

Jessica shrugged, dug into her purse, and handed Elizabeth a few bottles and tubes. Within minutes, Elizabeth had added blusher, deeper lip gloss, and more mascara, liner, and shadow.

"Better, don't you think?" she asked Jessica, who sat there with her mouth slightly open. Elizabeth hardly ever wore that much makeup. "Now, what can I put on besides this—this tacky horror," she demanded, pulling the hospital gown away from her body.

"Your shirt, your favorite nightshirt! I brought it." Jessica frantically groped in the overnight bag. Triumphantly, she pulled something out of the bag. The well-worn white knit sleep shirt with the UCLA logo on it had always been Elizabeth's favorite. No matter how many times Jessica had told her that the shirt was definitely unsexy, Elizabeth had replied, "Relax, Jess. It's me, and I like it."

Elizabeth stared at the shirt. "You expect me to wear *that* with interns and doctors in and out of here all day? You've got to be kidding. Why didn't you bring me something sexier?" Elizabeth asked in what could only be described as a whiny voice.

"*You* want something sexier?" Jessica asked, stunned.

"Is there something wrong with that?"

"Hey, no! I think it's terrific. I'll bring something fantastic this afternoon, but you're stuck with the shirt until then."

"I guess this *thing* is all right for a visit from Todd," Elizabeth muttered. "Help me on with it."

A confused Jessica helped Elizabeth change. She was happy her sister was finally getting interested in the right kind of makeup and clothes, but she couldn't figure out the reason for the sudden switch.

"I'll go see if Todd's in the waiting room."

Jessica spotted Todd Wilkins immediately. The tall, broad-shouldered basketball player was pacing back and forth across the small waiting room.

"Todd?"

"Jess, how is she?" he asked anxiously. "Is she all right? Does she hate me? Are you sure she wants to see me?"

"Slow down, Todd. Number one, she seems OK."

"*Seems?*"

"Will you *please* let me finish," Jessica said with a sigh of exasperation. "Liz is fine, really. You can only stay in there for ten or fifteen minutes, the doctor said, because she gets tired easily. And I'm sure she doesn't hate you, Todd."

"Something's wrong and you don't want to tell me."

"Nothing's wrong. She's going to be fine, just fine," Jessica said. "Go on in."

Todd peeked into Elizabeth's room. She was lying so still that at first he thought she was asleep. Then she opened her eyes and stared at him.

"Hello, Todd."

"Hi, how are you feeling?" Todd wanted to go to her and put his arms around her, but somehow he didn't dare.

"OK, I guess."

Todd walked to the side of the bed and reached for Elizabeth's hand.

"You look wonderful." A wave of guilt washed over him when he saw how fragile she looked.

I did this to her, he told himself. *How can she ever forgive me?*

"I thought basketball players had good eyesight, Todd," she said, pulling her hand from his to touch her hair. "On a scale of one to ten, I'm not even on the scale yet."

"You're always a ten to me, Liz," he quickly assured her. "About the accident . . ."

"I don't want to talk about it."

"I just wanted to tell you how terrible I feel and—"

"It's in the past, Todd. Let's just forget about it, OK?" Instead of looking at him, she focused her attention on her hands, which were restlessly plucking at the blanket.

"I don't want to upset you, Liz, but—"

"Todd, I'm really very tired." Elizabeth sighed and closed her eyes.

"Oh, gee—I'm sorry, Liz. I mean, I know I'm being inconsiderate. You need your rest. I'll get out of here right now."

When Todd came back out into the hall, Jessica was standing there with Dr. Edwards.

"If you two will excuse me," the doctor said, "I'll go in and check on my patient."

"Well, how *was* she?" Jessica asked impatiently as soon as she and Todd were alone.

"OK, I guess. Very quiet. She hardly said a word to me."

"She's exhausted, for heaven's sake."

"She said she was. But it almost seemed like she was bored—like she couldn't wait for me to leave."

"Guys are really something!" Jessica said angrily. "Liz just came out of a coma, and you expect her to be laughing and smiling as if nothing happened."

Just then the sound of Elizabeth's laughter floated out to the hall.

"Yeah, Jess, and then again, maybe doctors are more interesting than basketball players." Todd strode over to the elevator and punched the down button.

Jessica tiptoed to the door of Elizabeth's room and peeked in. Elizabeth looked anything but tired. Not only was she sitting up, she was smiling at Dr. Edwards. If she hadn't known that Elizabeth wasn't the flirting type, Jessica would have sworn her sister was making a play for the doctor.

Three weeks after the accident, Elizabeth was released from the hospital with orders from Dr. Edwards to rest at home for at least two weeks before returning to school.

Elizabeth laughed as she walked into the house and saw the living room decorated with streamers, balloons, and a giant banner that read, "Welcome Home, Liz."

"This has got to be your doing, Jess," she accused.

"Guilty as charged," Jessica said and laughed. "Do you like it?"

"Jess was up most of the night making the banner," Alice Wakefield said, giving Jessica a hug.

"And she got me to blow up the balloons," Ned Wakefield added. "She said it had something to do with lawyers being full of hot air."

"You don't think I overdid it, do you?" Jessica asked. "I wanted your homecoming to be special."

"You, Jessica Wakefield, overdo anything? Such a ridiculous thought never crossed my mind," Elizabeth teased.

"I could have gotten the marching band and the cheerleading squad to come over."

"Now *that* would have been overdoing it."

Alice Wakefield put her arm around her daughter's shoulder. "I think it's time we got you up to bed, honey."

"Don't bug me about rest, Mom," Elizabeth said.

"The doctor said—"

"Oh, all right," Elizabeth grumbled as she went up the stairs with her mother.

Jessica turned a worried face toward her father.

"Don't worry, Jess," he reassured her. "Liz just needs time to recover, that's all."

*   *   *

"Boring, boring, boring!" Jessica heard her sister complain as she was coming in to see Elizabeth after school.

"Don't tell me all this rest and relaxation is getting to you, Liz. I'll be glad to trade places with you—especially during science class," Jessica said and laughed.

"Nothing is more boring than five straight days of soaps and game shows," Elizabeth muttered.

"How about those books over there?" Jessica said, pointing at the stack of paperbacks on Elizabeth's writing table. "You've always said you wanted more time to read."

"That's supposed to be fun?" Elizabeth snapped.

"Hey, don't get bent out of shape, Liz. Reading isn't *my* idea of fun, but you always said you liked it."

"Maybe it's time I did less reading and more living, Jess. What do you think?"

Jessica cocked her head to one side and tapped it with the heel of her hand, like a swimmer trying to get the water out of her ears.

"I think I'm not hearing right. Are you sure you're my work-first-play-later twin sister, the very same sister who tells *me* to study *more?*"

"Oh, come on, Jessica, you make me sound

like some kind of creep," Elizabeth said, punching her pillow. "I've been taking it slowly ever since I got out of the hospital. I'm more than ready for some fun. After being bored out of my skull with television for five days, I've come up with an idea. A party! That's what we need. That's what *I* need."

"Great! But wait a minute, Liz, you can't go to a party, not yet anyway."

"One more week, Jess, that's all. Then I'll be out on parole, so then comes the party, OK?"

"Yeah, yeah, let me think a minute." Jessica walked around the room, her hands stuck in the back pockets of her jeans. "I heard Lila Fowler is thinking of having a party. I'll talk to her tomorrow."

"Forget Lila. I'm talking about *our* party, Jess."

"Ours?"

"Why not? We haven't had a pool party in months. Mom and Dad are sure to go along with it. We could tell them it would be—what's that medical term you used?"

"Therapeutic?"

"That's right. A party would be therapeutic for me."

Jessica couldn't have been happier. For a change she and Elizabeth seemed to want the same kind of fun. "I love it, Liz. I really love it. We'll invite every terrific guy we know. It'll be great." She began planning instantly. "Now, which girls do we invite, Liz? Lila and Cara Walker, of course," Jessica said, naming two of their Pi Beta Alpha sorority sisters. "And I suppose *you'll* want to include Enid Rollins."

"Why invite any of them, Jess? Can't the Wakefield sisters handle all those guys by themselves?"

Three

"Huh?" Jessica couldn't believe her ears. "Liz, you can't be serious. There's no way we could do that."

"Why not?"

"Well, because . . ." Jessica tried to think of a reason. Actually, she thought, that was the kind of party she'd always wanted. But certainly not the kind Elizabeth ever had. Then common sense caught up with Jessica. "We can't do it because every girl we know would hate us, Liz. And they'd stop inviting us to their parties. Guys almost never give parties, so we'd be out in the cold. Right?"

"OK, we'll invite some girls," Elizabeth conceded.

Jessica stared at her sister. There *was* something different about her. But what was it? Jessica peered closer. It *was* her twin sister sitting there on the bed, although she had traded in her UCLA nightshirt for a sexy satin nightgown.

"Why are you staring at me as if I've suddenly grown another head?" Elizabeth demanded.

"I was just wondering if Todd's seen you in that nightgown. I bet it'd raise his temperature about a hundred and thirty-seven degrees!"

"No, he hasn't! And he's not likely to," Elizabeth said angrily.

"Why not, for heaven's sake? If a guy *I* liked came to see *me* in my sickbed, I'd sure make the most of it." Jessica sighed dramatically, placed the back of her right hand on her forehead, and intoned, "Dahling, so good of you to come when I am at death's door!"

Mimicking Jessica, Elizabeth put her own hand to her head. She giggled. "That's a great line, Jess. I'll have to use it sometime."

"Oh, Liz, it is *so* terrific having you home again," Jessica said, giggling herself. "I never have as much fun with anyone else. Besides, in a week you'll be well enough to do *your* share of the dishes and the vacuuming and all the other boring chores I've been stuck with for the past lifetime and a half." She said the words with a grin, but Jessica was only half kidding. Even though doing dishes usually involved nothing more strenuous than loading and unloading the dishwasher, she was always looking for excuses to avoid her turn at it.

Elizabeth raised her right hand and in her most serious voice said, "I solemnly swear to take over my share of the chores as soon as I have made a total recovery—which should be in about three months!"

"What!"

Elizabeth smiled mischievously.

Jessica was about to give Elizabeth a snappy answer when she heard the chimes of the front doorbell. She scrambled off the bed and started for the door. "I'll bet *that* is the star of the Sweet Valley High basketball team. He said he was going to come over this afternoon."

"Todd is coming over here?"

"Yeah. Fix your face. I'll bring him right up."

"No!"

Jessica looked at her sister in amazement. "You don't want to see Todd?"

"No. Tell him I'm too tired to see anyone. Tell him I'll see him when I'm allowed to go back to school."

"Well, if you're sure. . . ."

Elizabeth's eyes were already closed. She did look tired, Jessica thought.

Jessica hurried down the stairs as the chimes sounded again. "I'm coming, I'm coming," she called.

She swung the door open and found Todd standing in the doorway.

27

"Hi, Jess. Can I see—"

"Shush," she whispered. "Into the kitchen."

Todd followed her through the large, airy living room and dining room to the kitchen at the back of the house.

"Why are you shushing me, Jess? Is something wrong?"

"No, of course not. It's just that Liz is sleeping. She can't have any visitors."

"She's all right, isn't she?" Jessica saw the look of worry on Todd's face.

"She's fine. But can't you understand that she's *tired*? She's been through so much in the past few weeks."

"Yes, but she seemed so different when I saw her in the hospital, as if something were wrong. I know she's tired and the doctors say she's all right—physically. But the accident was a nightmare. It must have been terrible for her."

"You're absolutely right, Todd. It was just awful. And that's why she needs as much rest as she can get, as few people bothering her as possible."

"Then she does remember the accident?"

"Oh, sure," Jessica said, not quite certain if that were true.

Todd's expression was haggard. "Does it haunt her, Jessica? Does she blame me? Jessica, does she ever ask for me?"

"Oh, Todd, she's too busy getting well to ask for *anyone* yet."

Todd's face fell. Then he looked straight at Jessica. "Tell me, do *you* think anything is different about Liz?"

"Todd Wilkins, don't talk like a jerk! Of course nothing's different. She's my twin sister, and I'd notice if there were. She's absolutely fine."

"I hope you're right, Jess." Todd got up and paced back and forth across the kitchen floor, uncertain what to do next. Finally he walked to the back door. "Tell Liz I'll stop by tomorrow afternoon, will you? Maybe she'll feel better then."

"Don't do that, Todd."

"Huh?"

Elizabeth always knew how to break bad news to people without making them feel rotten, Jessica thought. That was because she could understand how they were feeling. *But I'm not that way*, Jessica said to herself. *How does she do it?*

Crossing her fingers under the table, Jessica said, "My folks have decided that Liz shouldn't have any visitors until she's ready to go back to school."

"But that's over a week," Todd protested.

"Orders are orders," Jessica insisted. "Once Liz gets back to school, everything will return to normal. You know how much she likes school. She'll probably have all the work made up and a dozen stories written for *The Oracle* before I finish that one stupid book report on *Moby Dick*.

I mean, Todd, who really cares about whales?" Jessica asked in annoyance.

Todd did, but he let the comment slide by. For the first time that afternoon, he smiled. "You're right, Jess, I am being a jerk. When Liz gets back to school, everything will be terrific again. I mean, Liz is really something. She's smart, she's hardworking, she's a good writer, she's nice to everybody—and she's beautiful!"

Todd suddenly stopped talking and looked at Jessica, who was grinning up at him. He had forgotten for a few moments that he had an audience. Embarrassed, he mumbled, "You're her twin, so I guess that makes you beautiful, too."

"Thanks a heap, Todd," she said, still grinning. "Why don't you get out of here now and go bounce a basketball or something? I have to get dinner started."

Jessica watched Todd's tall, lean form disappear around the corner of the house and thought how curious life could be sometimes. Who would have thought the two of them would ever be able to talk together like friends? They had been barely civil to each other ever since she'd tried to steal Todd away from her sister. Now they had a common cause—helping Elizabeth.

The sharp ring of the telephone interrupted Jessica's thoughts. She picked up the kitchen extension.

"Hello? Oh, hi, Mom." Jessica wound a strand

of hair around her finger as she listened to her mother.

"Yes, Mom. Liz is fine. . . . Yes, I'm fine, too. . . . Of course I've already started dinner. Didn't I promise I would? 'Bye."

For the next twenty minutes, Jessica rushed from refrigerator to counter to pantry to oven in a frantic effort to get dinner ready on time. "How did Liz do it?" she muttered, remembering that her sister had almost always been the one to start dinner. But that was before the accident.

"Hey, you almost ready?" Jessica asked, coming into Elizabeth's room. "This is the big day. You—"

Jessica completely forgot what she was going to say when she got a look at her sister standing in front of the full-length mirror.

"Freedom day, Jess, that's what it is. How do I look?" she asked, turning around.

"Terrific, Liz, really terrific," she said, eyeing her sister's green minidress with envy. "Where'd the new outfit come from?"

"Mom let me pick out a 'return to the world' dress. And get that look out of your eye, Jessica. This is definitely not borrowable."

"Why in the world would you think—?"

"Because I know you, sister dear," Elizabeth answered, grinning. "Hands off."

Jessica looked at her own reflection in the mirror. The jeans and shirt had looked great five minutes ago. Now they looked dull and uninteresting.

Throughout breakfast, Elizabeth was subdued. She smiled and said "yes" every time her mother and father asked her if she felt well enough to return to school. During the ride to the Sweet Valley High campus, she nodded and smiled occasionally as Jessica kept up a steady stream of chatter. Jessica was in great spirits, as she always was when she was allowed to drive the little red Fiat Spider to school.

"You're not nervous, are you, Liz?" she asked. "I mean, it's not like you've been gone for years. It's only been a few weeks. You won't have any trouble catching up," she assured her sister.

"Jess, you're beginning to bug me." Elizabeth snapped. "I am fine. I am not nervous. I am not worried about catching up—or anything else!"

"Of course you're not," Jessica said quickly, realizing she was the one who was nervous. She wanted everything to go perfectly for her sister that day. It just had to.

Jessica pulled the car into a spot in the student parking lot with her usual flourish. She halfway expected Elizabeth to tell her to stop showing off, but Elizabeth got out of the car without giving the expected lecture on safe driving.

At that moment Enid Rollins dashed over to

welcome her best friend back to school. Her large green eyes glowed happily, lighting up her whole face.

"Liz!" she cried, throwing her arms around Jessica. "I've been dying to talk to you, but Todd said you couldn't have visitors or telephone calls. It's so great to see you! You look terrific!"

"Enid, you are about to choke me, for heaven's sake," Jessica said, pulling away. "You are really dumb, you know that? I'm *Jessica*, can't you tell?"

Enid dropped her arms quickly. "But I thought you were—" she hesitated. "Where's Liz?"

"There she goes," Jessica said, pointing to the figure in green hurrying across the wide front lawn. Elizabeth waved to friends as she made her way quickly under the columns and through the front entrance of the school building.

She decided she had enough time to check in at *The Oracle* before her first class. As she walked into the cluttered newspaper office, Roger Collins, the good-looking young teacher who served as the paper's adviser, was relaxing over a cup of coffee. He looked up with a smile that quickly became a frown.

"Jessica, I certainly hope you're not here to tell me Elizabeth still isn't well enough to come to school."

"Mr. Collins, we just may have to get your eyes checked out," Elizabeth teased. "Don't you recognize your ace reporter, the distinguished author of 'Eyes and Ears'?''

Mr. Collins's jaw dropped slightly. "Elizabeth?"

"Elizabeth," she confirmed, dropping gracefully into a chair.

"Well, maybe a little knock on the head would be good for all of us," he said. "You look wonderful, and I'm glad to have you back. We all missed you."

"You look pretty good, too," Elizabeth said. Every girl at Sweet Valley High would have agreed with her. Roger Collins wasn't the most popular teacher at school only because he was interesting in class. In fact, most of the girls would have loved a little after-class attention from this teacher.

"Believe it or not, Mr. Collins," Elizabeth continued, "I missed this dusty old room and all the last-minute deadline hysteria."

"Well, it's still here, exactly the way you left it." Then he turned serious. "Being in the hospital must have been a horrible ordeal," he said.

"Not all of it was bad." She gave him a dazzling smile. "Fowler Hospital has some fantastic-looking doctors and interns. And some of the nurses aren't at all bad, in case *you're* interested."

For the second time that morning, Mr. Collins's jaw dropped in surprise.

"Just a suggestion, Mr. Collins," Elizabeth said and grinned. "I'd better go now. I don't

want to be late for my first class. See you later!"
And she was gone.

"See you. Welcome back, *Elizabeth*?" he questioned faintly.

Mr. Collins wasn't the only confused one at Sweet Valley High that day. Other teachers and many of the kids kept mistaking Elizabeth for Jessica. None of this bothered Elizabeth at all, but Jessica was beginning to have an identity crisis.

The rest of the week wasn't much different from that first day. Elizabeth didn't wear the green minidress again, but she showed up in one new outfit after another.

"Mom must have bought you an entire new wardrobe," Jessica said with a trace of envy.

"Just a few things I needed, Jess. And you're a fine one to talk. You've always wrangled more clothes out of her than I did."

"But you never wanted them," she pointed out.

"I do now."

Why don't I like the sound of that? Jessica asked herself. The only thing that kept Jessica going that week was the thought of the pool party she and Elizabeth were throwing on Saturday night.

She spent Saturday afternoon at the beach, playing volleyball with the kids, working on her tan, and feeling sorry for everyone who didn't live in Southern California. She was also feeling sorry for Todd Wilkins, who wasn't having any fun at the beach.

"I thought Liz would be coming with you today, Jess."

"She's home resting up for tonight's party. She's still kind of weak, you know."

"Oh."

"Why the long face, Todd?"

Todd squinted up at the bright sun for a moment, then shrugged his broad shoulders. "I just never seem to get a chance to be alone with Liz. Every time I've seen her this past week, she's been too busy to talk."

"Well, she *is* busy, for heaven's sake. Liz has a lot of catching up to do."

"I guess you're right, but I wish—"

Jessica shook her head in exasperation. "Of course I'm right. You'll have plenty of time to be alone with her tonight."

The thought of being alone with Elizabeth brought a smile to Todd's face. "Yeah, tonight will be great."

Jessica hummed happily as she came into the kitchen late that afternoon. Alice and Ned Wakefield would be out the rest of the day and evening but had given their daughters special permission to have a party without their supervision. "We know we can trust you," they'd said.

Jessica was wondering whether she should go up and wake Elizabeth when the phone rang.

"Hello?"

"Hi, Jess, it's me."

"Liz? I thought you were upstairs."

"I'm at the mall, Jess. Please don't be mad, but I remembered something vitally important I had to do."

Jessica drummed her fingers impatiently on the counter as she listened. "You're at the mall? I'm not mad, Liz, but you're supposed to be up in your room resting for the party."

"I'll be home soon, I promise!"

"How soon, Liz? There's a lot of work to be done before the kids get here." The fingers were still drumming.

"Not to worry, Jess. I'll be there in a flash. Why don't you start things?" And the line went dead.

"Well, how do you like that? She wants *me* to start the work!"

Four

Jessica kept telling herself she shouldn't be upset with Elizabeth. After all, she thought, Elizabeth was just getting back on her feet. So, OK, she had left her with all the work of setting up for the party. "Listen, Jessica Wakefield," she lectured herself, "haven't you ever ducked out on work and left Elizabeth to do it?" She sighed and got out the onion soup mix to make the dip.

Actually, that was just the trouble. Normally it would have been Jessica calling from the mall to say she'd be late and for Elizabeth to go ahead setting things up without her. This just was not like Elizabeth.

"Now, don't start creating a humungous, imaginary crisis over nothing," she cautioned herself aloud. "Knowing my sister, she might even be picking up some wonderful surprise for the party."

Still, it nagged at her.

"Stop it," Jessica commanded herself. "If you don't make that dip, the kids will have to eat powdered soup mix." She giggled and kept working.

Jessica checked the pool, skimming out leaves and twigs, and made sure the chlorine level was right. She set out the chips and dip and lugged the ice chest filled with soda out onto the patio. Then she moved the stereo speakers.

Pausing to look in a mirror, she reacted with horror. "Yaaaaagh," she gagged, looking at her tangled hair and red, sweaty face.

That was the problem with doing all the work. You wound up red-faced, sweaty, cross, and tired. Jessica made one last circuit of the patio, going around the pool to check the little wrought-iron tables, and then raced inside to take a shower.

"Hey!" she yelled in surprise when she got upstairs. She heard the sound of the shower running. "Is that you, Liz?"

"In a minute," she heard floating out from the volcano of steam and froth in the shower.

"Well, how do you like *that*?" Jessica muttered. Elizabeth had come home, done nothing to help, and sailed into the shower first!

"Elizabeth Wakefield, you come out of there!" Jessica raged.

"What?" said Elizabeth, turning off the shower, wrapping a towel around herself, then jumping out and smiling radiantly at Jessica. "Isn't this going to be a great party?"

Jessica stood there glaring, but Elizabeth didn't seem to notice. She just skipped past and darted into her room, looking back out to say, "Hey, Jess, you'd better get a move on. You're an absolute mess."

Jessica threw up her hands, got undressed, then went into the shower.

By the time Jessica put on her ice-blue bikini for the pool party, Elizabeth was already out of her room.

"Liz," Jessica called out. "You there?" No answer.

Jessica checked herself out in the mirror, examining her slim, perfectly tanned figure and her smashingly daring bikini. She smiled. "Not bad," she murmured. The boys of Sweet Valley wouldn't have a chance that night.

By the time she came downstairs, the gang was already starting to arrive. Gathered around the pool were Cara Walker, Lila Fowler, and Enid Rollins, Todd Wilkins and Ken Matthews, the football captain, John Pfeifer from *The Oracle*, and even crazy Winston Egbert with his new girlfriend, Mandy Farmer. They were all standing around somebody near the diving board, somebody who had their undivided attention.

Jessica heard a provocative, flirtatious laugh

rise from the circle of boys. "That's *my* laugh," she whispered, confused. But it was Elizabeth doing the laughing.

Jessica strolled over for a closer look, and her eyes almost popped out. It was Elizabeth, all right, but she wasn't wearing her old swimsuit. She looked simply sensational in a brand-new, very revealing green bikini. It sure wasn't Elizabeth's usual style.

It wasn't only the new bikini, which Elizabeth had bought at the mall while Jessica slaved away like Cinderella. No, it was something in the way Elizabeth moved among the awed guys. She was holding a platter of chips and dip, and as she turned between Ken Matthews and John Pfeifer, she treated each of them to dazzling smiles.

Jessica sensed someone standing beside her, and looking around, saw it was Todd. He was gazing at Elizabeth with an odd expression on his face. He looked at Jessica. She looked at him. They glanced back toward Elizabeth.

"Well, I guess she's feeling better," Todd said with an effort, looking for something positive in this strange behavior.

"If she felt any better, she'd be orbiting the moon," muttered Jessica.

But Jessica couldn't really complain. She was glad to see Elizabeth enjoying herself so much. The party was a blazing success, largely because of Elizabeth's radiant performance. She picked out the music, insisted on dancing with every boy, and kept up a nonstop chatter that the guys found fascinating.

Jessica and Todd stood by the patio doors drinking sodas and watching the new firefly of the Wakefield family.

Todd sighed. "It's terrific to see her so happy," he said, though his hopes of being alone with Elizabeth were rapidly disappearing.

"Yeah. She's so happy she doesn't notice we're out of chips, ice cubes, and soda," Jessica said.

It was weird. At parties Jessica was always the one who whirled and sparkled while Elizabeth kept the food coming. Now Jessica was doing all the work.

Just then Winston Egbert came up. "Kind princess, something to wet my parched throat before I expire, please! And a drink for my lady."

Jessica felt a curious twinge of jealousy. She knew Winston had been crazy about *her* since grade school, and usually she couldn't be bothered with him. But tonight was different. He was just about the only boy at the party *not* hanging all over Elizabeth. There was only one problem. He wasn't paying attention to anyone except Mandy.

"Hang in there, Win. I'll get more soda for you and Mandy," Jessica said, heading back toward the house.

When Jessica returned, she spotted Elizabeth

standing in front of Ken Matthews, gazing soulfully into his eyes, as though hypnotized by whatever magic words he was saying. When she got close enough, she heard their conversation with amazement.

"I was just telling my father the other day, Ken Matthews knows all there is to know about football."

"Well . . ." Ken blushed.

"Oh, yes, you do, Ken. Why, I bet we'll see you out there playing with the Rams in a few years."

Jessica stood there, holding the tray of soda cans. Elizabeth Wakefield playing up to Ken Matthews? Impossible! *She's just being friendly, just being a good hostess,* Jessica told herself. *So what if she's having more fun than I am? She deserves it.* Jessica put the tray on a table and walked over to where Todd was sitting alone.

"Jess, have you been watching Liz?" he said cautiously. "Does she seem different to you?"

"What? No," said Jessica. "She seems really terrific tonight."

"Yeah, terrific with everybody but me."

"You're jealous!" she accused. "And you're mad because she's having a fantastic time, and the two of us are just—"

"Yes, Jess, the *two* of us. It occurs to me that you're just a little miffed at your sister for stealing your usual place in the spotlight."

43

"Todd, really, you can be an awful nerd sometimes," she said and stalked away.

Todd was wrong, she told herself. She wasn't the sort of person who always had to be the center of attention, was she? And neither was Elizabeth—at least not before that night.

Things began adding up in a way Jessica didn't like. But there it was. Elizabeth had conveniently gone shopping at the mall instead of being home to help with the party preparations. The Elizabeth Jessica had always known would never have done that. Elizabeth had told her she had something vitally important to do at the mall. And what was that? Buying a new bikini! Not only had she gotten out of setting up for the party, but she'd also sneaked home and into the shower right under her sister's nose. And finally, there was Elizabeth, looking sensational, flirting madly with every guy at the party.

Why, she's doing at least a hundred and thirty-seven things that I usually do, Jessica raged inwardly. *At least, things I sometimes do. Once in a while.*

She was so busy thinking that she might actually have walked blindly into the pool if she hadn't bumped into Cara Walker.

Cara turned, saw the tray of sodas Jessica was carrying, and took a can.

"Well," said Cara, looking over her shoulder toward the other end of the swimming pool, where Elizabeth was surrounded by five guys, "would you check out Miss Butterfly of the Year?"

"What kind of a crack is that?" Jessica snapped. "Isn't my sister allowed to have a good time?"

Cara apologized quickly. "I'm sorry, Jess. I didn't mean anything by it. It's just that I've watched you in action with guys and—"

"What?"

Cara's face turned beet red. Her apology was only making things worse, and she knew Jessica was getting mad at her. "Jess, you always know the right thing to do around guys. You're really terrific in everything, especially cheerleading, and you're a marvelous dancer, and you—"

"Calm down, Cara," Jessica said, then sighed. Usually she liked Cara telling her how terrific she was, but tonight she had other things on her mind.

"What I was trying to say was that I've never seen *Liz* in action. She's always friendly, but not *this* friendly. I thought she only had eyes for Todd, but tonight she's breaking all records for flirting."

Jessica hardly knew what to say, she was so angry. "My sister is not a flirt!"

"OK, OK. But she certainly seems different."

"She is not," Jessica snapped angrily. "She's been under a lot of tension lately, but she is *not* different. She's exactly the same."

Jessica walked away from Cara, trying to convince herself that what she had said was the truth. But she was afraid it wasn't.

Cara Walker had unwittingly suggested what was bothering Jessica most. She had been circling around it all evening, feeling it, but unwilling to say or even think it.

Elizabeth had somehow turned into her, Jessica! She was even out-Jessica-ing her. It couldn't happen. It must not be allowed to happen.

If she's Jessica, she agonized, *then who am I?*

She chased the confusing thoughts out of her mind by hurrying around and taking care of the party. She became a demon at work, getting ice cubes, cleaning tables, mopping spilled sodas. Keeping busy helped a lot. Still, every time she passed Elizabeth, she was startled all over again to see the lively, glowing face of her sister lighting up the party.

By the end of the party, everyone was looking at Jessica and Elizabeth and whispering. Everyone knew something was wrong.

Everyone, that is, except Elizabeth. She chattered on brilliantly and unknowingly until the last.

What seemed to Jessica like a million years later, the party finally ended. When the last person had left, she closed the front door and turned to her sister. "Liz," she said. "I want to talk to you."

Elizabeth's eyes fluttered. "Jessie, is my face flushed?"

"What?"

"I guess it's nothing. I seem to have the most horrible headache coming on."

Jessica felt alarm growing inside her. She wondered if Elizabeth was having a relapse. "What's the matter, Lizzie?" she asked quickly.

"It's probably nothing. I just feel a little woozy."

"Oh, please, go lie down," said Jessica.

"Well, maybe I'd better—if you don't mind," said Elizabeth, and the next moment she shot up the stairs two at a time.

Jessica hurried around the pool and the patio, cleaning things up. *I hope she's all right*, she thought.

It wasn't until she was almost finished that Jessica realized she had done *all* the work for the party. She had set up, dashed around like a servant all evening, and then cleaned everything afterward.

The only thing Elizabeth had done was decide to have the party.

Stop it, she told herself. Elizabeth would have done the same thing for her. She was just tired.

Sure, said another inner voice. *She was really a decrepit wreck when she hopped up the stairs like a little rabbit about two seconds after saying she had a splitting headache.* Every time there'd been work

47

to do that day, Elizabeth had developed a sudden problem.

Jessica understood all these tricks well enough because she had used every one of them time and again on her sister.

And then she froze. The same frightening sensation swept through her. "Is it possible? Has Elizabeth turned into me?"

Five

Jessica let herself in through the back door, relieved to be home. It had been one crazy day—all of it bad. She'd be lucky to get a decent grade on her English test, but that wasn't what was really upsetting her. Being unprepared for a test was not unusual for her. But it was for Elizabeth, and Jessica was sure her sister hadn't cracked a book all week.

"How could she have time for studying when she's on the phone with guys most of the time?" she asked herself aloud. "Then of course there has to be time for manicures, pedicures, doing her hair—" She stopped herself in midsentence and glanced around the empty kitchen.

"I'm talking to myself," she said in amazement. "I'm coming so unglued that I am actually talking to myself." She poured a tall glass of orange

49

juice. "What I should be doing is talking to somebody else about Liz. But who?"

Todd? No, he was still at basketball practice. Their parents? They hadn't seen Elizabeth in action at the pool party the week before, and besides, Jessica didn't want to worry them.

Steven! she thought, reaching for the wall phone. Big brother to the rescue, right? Wrong. Jessica hung up the phone without dialing her brother's number at the university.

What in the world would she say to him? "Hey, Steve, Liz is flirting with every good-looking guy in Sweet Valley. Do something about it." She groaned. He'd just accuse her of being jealous. So would anyone else, for that matter.

But Jessica knew jealousy wasn't the problem. There was no longer any doubt in her mind. Elizabeth had changed. *It's my fault*, Jessica admitted. *I was thoughtless and selfish the night of Enid's party, and because of that, Elizabeth got hurt, spent all that time in the hospital, and now this. And not just at Enid's. I was always selfish. I acted just like—Elizabeth's acting now!*

Just then Elizabeth slammed the back door, stomped across the floor, scuffing its shiny surface with her boot heels, and tossed her books on the table. "What an absolutely gruesome day!" she said, frowning fiercely.

Jessica stared at her, fascinated.

"If all you're going to do is stare at me, take your face someplace else!"

50

"I didn't mean to stare, Liz. I was just—"

"Staring!"

"Look, I don't mean to butt in, but I really think you ought to slow down a bit."

"Slow down? You've got to be kidding. You've been telling me for years that I've been hanging out with kids so dull that you need No-Doz just to be in the same room with them. You were right, Jess. From now on, thanks to you, I'm living in the fast lane!" Elizabeth dashed out of the room. "Got to change," she called over her shoulder.

"Did you hear that, Dr. Frankenstein?" Jessica muttered. "You're not the only one who created a monster."

"Thanks, honey. You can take the salad in." Alice Wakefield smiled at Elizabeth's retreating back and turned to Jessica.

"Isn't it wonderful to have Liz at home again?"

"Yeah, sure, Mom," Jessica answered.

Talk at the dinner table that night was light. Alice Wakefield asked the girls how things were at school.

"Just fine," Elizabeth said in a soft voice.

Jessica nearly choked on a cherry tomato.

"Jessica, are you all right?" Her father began pounding her on her back.

"Yeah, I suppose," she finally croaked. Privately, she thought she'd never be all right again.

Everyone knew Elizabeth was in trouble at school. Everyone except her parents, that is.

Jessica was still thinking about her sister when Ned Wakefield dropped the bombshell.

"The Percys are going to be in Europe for a few weeks for some kind of computer conference, and we're going to have some houseguests," he said brightly. Alice Wakefield nodded in agreement.

The Percys? Jessica frowned. Weren't they the ones with—

"The Percys' twelve-year-old twin girls are going to stay with us while their parents are away," her father said. "Won't that be fun?"

An openmouthed Jessica stared at her father.

"Fun?" Elizabeth sputtered. "A broken leg would be more fun than baby-sitting those two little twerps."

Alice Wakefield gave her daughter a look of surprise. "Elizabeth, I hardly expected—"

"Hey, Liz," Jessica jumped in quickly. "It won't be so bad. Like having kid sisters in a way. We'll let them do all our chores."

"Jessica!"

"Kidding, Mom. Just kidding, honest."

"That's my girl." Ned Wakefield beamed.

Jessica didn't know whether to laugh or scream. She certainly didn't want those two little brats around. But she'd pulled a perfect Elizabeth by sticking up for them.

Finally, Elizabeth said, "If Jess can cope with them, I guess I can, too."

The Wakefield parents exchanged proud smiles.

"You girls always come through for us," Alice said. "To show my appreciation, I'll clean up the kitchen tonight. Why don't you girls get an early start on your homework while your father goes over to the Percys' to pick up the twins?"

Half an hour later, Elizabeth and Jessica came back downstairs to meet the Percy twins. Although the Percys were friends of their parents, Elizabeth and Jessica had never met them. The twins were fragile, dark-haired girls with large brown eyes set in small, solemn faces. They were wearing identical gray jumpers and long-sleeved white blouses, and they were clutching identical black flute cases.

Jessica took one look at them and decided to move to San Francisco at the earliest possible moment. She plastered a smile on her face and said, "Hi." She had to strain her ears to hear them answer softly, in unison, "Hello."

Elizabeth muttered something that sounded like "Hello," then excused herself, muttering something else that sounded like "Homework."

As soon as the Percy twins were settled in Steven's room, Ned and Alice Wakefield left for an evening of bridge.

While the twins were unpacking, Jessica finally got a moment alone with Elizabeth. "Liz, I know this is going to be a real bummer. But we can handle it, right?" *Liz, please say right!*

"You've got to be kidding, Jess." Elizabeth's eyes flashed with anger. "Can you believe those two? And their names, Jean and Joan. Their parents must be real morons."

"We *can* do it, Liz," Jessica insisted. "Remember what you've always told me? When we work together, we can do anything."

"I said that?"

"Sure." *She must have said it*, Jessica thought. It sounded just like something Elizabeth would have said—once.

"OK, Jess, we'll work together, I guess."

Jessica hugged her in relief. "Terrific, Liz. Did I tell you about my absolutely sensational plans for tonight? I'm giving Danny Stauffer a second chance. He's taking me to the drive-in!"

"What's playing?"

"Who cares? Did I ever tell you about the front seat in Danny's car? It slides back and reclines and—and I probably don't have to draw you a picture, do I?"

"No, Jess, pictures aren't necessary. Have fun," she added, going into her room.

Happy and relieved, Jessica went to get ready for what she knew was going to be a memorable evening. She would have been anything but happy if she'd known what was going on in Elizabeth's room.

As Jessica changed into black pants and a

low-cut blouse, Elizabeth was slipping into a new miniskirt even shorter than the green one that hung in her closet. Fifteen minutes later she checked herself out in the full-length mirror. Her blue-green eyes glowed sexily, emphasized by perfect makeup. Her long, sun-streaked blond hair swung gracefully around her shoulders.

"Not bad, Liz," she said aloud. "Not bad at all."

As she stepped out into the hall, she carefully stepped over the extra-long phone cord. Jessica had carried the hallway phone into her room, and Elizabeth could hear Jessica saying, "Ohhhh, Danny, do you really think we could do *that*?" Her voice was very breathy.

Elizabeth went down the hall to Steven's room and stuck her head in the doorway. The quiet Percy twins had finished unpacking and were sitting on the bed.

"Hi, kids, how are you doing?"

"Fine," they said in unison.

"Great. I thought my mom might be in here, but I guess she's downstairs."

"She went out," Jean said.

"With your father to play bridge," Joan added.

"Darn! I forgot all about that."

"Are you going to stay with us?"

"Me? No!" Softening her voice a little, she explained. "I have a date. And so does Jess," she added in a whisper.

Jean and Joan looked at each other with a

combination of confusion and panic. Were they going to be left alone their first night in a strange house?

"Hey, don't worry. We'll think of something. Come on." Without a word the Percy twins followed Elizabeth into the hall and down the stairs into the living room.

"Look, kids, Jess is going to the movies tonight. Do you like drive-ins?"

Joan and Jean nodded solemnly.

"She won't mind if you tag along with her, OK?"

More nods.

Elizabeth started for the front door, then stopped. "One more thing. Tell Jessica I'm really sorry and that I'll make it up to her." As she went out the door, she said, "Tell Jess that something vitally important came up."

Six

Jessica hummed as she put the finishing touches on her makeup. She added a bit more blusher and lip gloss and then looked critically at her face in the mirror. The twenty minutes she had spent doing her eyes had been worth it.

She checked the way her black pants and red blouse showed off her slender figure. "Good thing you lost those two pounds, Jess," she told herself. "Dan wouldn't want to put his arms around a blimpo."

Then she grabbed her purse and sailed out of the room. As she went past Elizabeth's room, Jessica felt a twinge of guilt. She shouldn't be sticking Elizabeth with the twins, she thought. But it had been so long since she'd had any fun. She'd make it up to her sister, she promised silently.

Jean and Joan Percy were sitting in the living room, just where Elizabeth had left them. As soon as she saw them, Jessica lost her happy smile and almost lost her temper. What in the world were those two little creeps doing in the living room when she had a date coming? They were definitely *not* part of the image she wanted to present to Danny.

"Well," she said. "Well, well." How quickly could she get rid of them? "Don't you have some homework to do?" she asked hopefully.

"There's no school tomorrow," said Jean.

"It's Saturday," said Joan.

"Great. Just my luck," Jessica said. "Maybe you could get a head start on the work. It's not a good idea to leave studying to the last minute, you know." *And I should know*, she thought. *I do most of my studying five minutes before a test.*

When the girls didn't take her up on that suggestion, Jessica felt a touch of panic. She was determined to get them out of the living room before Danny arrived.

"Hey, kids, I've got it! You could go up to Liz's room and play whatever is in those little black cases for her. She really likes music. I mean, that would really make her night."

"Those are flutes," said Jean.

"Liz isn't in her room," said Joan.

"She's not? Where is she?" Before either twin could answer, Jessica came up with what she hoped was the right answer. "Oh, I see. She

58

must be in the kitchen fixing a snack for you. She's just great at that. That sister of mine is so sweet and thoughtful," she said. *And if she's not in the kitchen*, Jessica added to herself, *I will be violently ill immediately*.

"Liz went out," said Jean. "She said she had an important date."

"She said to tell you she was sorry and that she'd make it up to you," Joan added. "She said you'd take us to the movies tonight."

"She went *where*? She said *what*?" Jessica was stunned. It couldn't be happening to her. She didn't deserve this kind of treatment from her sister. It was a joke, that's what it was, an elaborate practical joke just to scare her.

Another look at those identical serious faces and Jessica knew that Elizabeth was not going to pop into the room shouting "Gotcha." It was a joke, all right, a deadly serious one.

"No, no, no," she said. "I've got plans for tonight, and they do not include a cast of thousands."

Her mind worked frantically as she paced back and forth across the room. A baby-sitter! That's it, hire a sitter! *Great, Jessica*, she told herself in disgust. *You've got exactly seventy-five cents. Not even the neighbor's dog would sit for wages like that*.

Jessica was ready to grab any sensible solution. Forget sensible—any solution at all would do.

"I bet you two have stayed at home without a

sitter lots of times." Hope was still alive in Jessica's heart.

Both girls shook their heads, their panic now as obvious as Jessica's.

Jessica considered and then immediately rejected the idea of leaving them on their own. Her parents would probably ground her until she was old enough to collect Social Security checks.

Never in all her sixteen years had Jessica Wakefield been so angry at her sister.

How could she do this to me? she raged silently. She knew Elizabeth had been sick, desperately sick. But Jessica had been patient and loving, hadn't she? And this was her reward?

How am I going to get out of this mess? she asked the ceiling. Just then the front doorbell rang.

"Oh, rats, he's here!" She looked wildly around the room, hoping a solution might pop out of thin air.

The doorbell sounded again.

"It's not fair. It's absolutely the most unfair thing that's ever happened to me in my entire life!" Jessica stormed as she opened the front door.

"Why, hello there." Even in the depths of despair, Jessica could always manage a dazzling smile.

Tall, good-looking Danny Stauffer stepped into

the foyer, returning the smile as he looked Jessica over.

"You're gorgeous, as usual," he said, putting his arms around her and kissing her on the mouth long and hard.

At that moment Jessica didn't care if the whole world were sitting in the living room with the Percy twins. Danny Stauffer knew how to kiss a girl better than any boy Jessica had ever dated. She melted into his arms for a second kiss.

"Jess," he murmured.

"Hmmmmmmm?" She wanted to prolong the kiss and the feeling of his strong body against hers.

"Jess," he said again, shaking her slightly. "I think we've got company." He was grinning and looking into the living room.

"Company? That's nice." She didn't move.

"There are two munchkins watching us. Maybe we'd better wait till we get to the drive-in."

Munchkins? Watching? Rats! They were still there.

"Oh!" *Think fast*, she told herself. "Look, Danny, there's been just a small change in tonight's plans. You're really going to freak out when you hear this. I mean, it's really the funniest thing."

"Funny? Funny like in ha-ha or funny like in strange?"

"Oh, it's funny ha-ha, I promise you." Taking a deep breath, she led him into the living room.

"These are the Percys. That's Jean, and that's Joan."

"She's Jean, I'm Joan."

"That's right. I'm Jean, she's Joan."

"Thanks for clearing that up," Jessica said through clenched teeth. Turning her brightest smile on Danny, she tried to explain the situation.

"You see, Danny, Jean and Joan, whichever one is which, are staying with us for a few weeks. My parents have gone out for the evening and so has my sister.

"So?"

"Soooo, they have to come with us to the drive-in."

Danny stepped back a little, looking at Jessica as if she were a candidate for the funny farm.

"Those two"—he gestured in the general direction of Jean and Joan—"Those two whatevers are going to come with us to the drive-in? I don't believe this!"

Jessica pulled him out of the twins' earshot and began speaking as fast as she could.

"Danny, please listen to me. It'll be all right, I promise you. Look at them. They're small, they're quiet, they hardly ever say a word. They'll fade right into the upholstery. Trust me!"

Danny didn't even bother looking at the twins again. He looked directly into Jessica's eyes and said, "No way, Jess. I told you what I had planned for tonight. There is no way I want an audience. I'm leaving." He started for the front door.

Jessica was desperate. If Danny left, she was not only stuck with the twerps for the night, she would probably never get another chance to go out with him.

"Danny, don't go!" She grabbed his arm. "Please don't go. It won't be so bad. They'll be in the backseat. We'll still be alone in the front."

"Whoopee." The look on his face was anything but friendly. "That's not what I had in mind."

"Danny," she said hesitantly. "I'll make it up to you."

"Make it up? How?"

Jessica knew she was getting in deeper than she wanted to, but she couldn't seem to stop herself. "Any way you want," she finally said.

"Yeah?"

"Yeah."

"OK! Let's go, munchkins. You don't look much like lucky charms, but that's what you're turning out to be."

Jessica scrawled a quick note to her parents and stuck it under a magnet on the refrigerator door before dashing off to get into the car with Danny and the twins.

Three misery-filled hours later, Jessica unlocked the front door for herself and Jean and Joan.

She knew it hadn't really been three hours. It had been three weeks or maybe even three centuries. She didn't want to see twins or movies or maybe even Danny Stauffer ever again. With any luck at all, she would die sometime during the night.

Just as she was going to send the twins upstairs, she saw her parents come out from the kitchen.

"Jess, we saw your note," her mother said. "How nice of you to take the twins out with you tonight. Did you have fun, girls?"

"Yes, thank you," they said in unison.

"Isn't that nice? You two better get up to your room. It's late. Sleep well."

Jessica watched in disbelief as they went quietly up the stairs. As a matter of fact, she regarded the whole evening with disbelief.

"Honey, I'm so proud of you," Alice Wakefield said.

Ned Wakefield put an arm around his daughter's shoulders. "We can always count on our little pumpkin, can't we?"

"Mom! Dad! This has positively been the grossest night of my life!" Jessica burst into tears of rage.

"Jessica, what's wrong?"

"Everything's wrong, Dad!"

Alice and Ned Wakefield exchanged questioning looks, and Jessica wondered if they were aware of what was going on under their very own roof.

"OK, for starters, Mom, those two little people who just went upstairs are not what they seem to be. Oh, boy, are they not what you think they are!" Jessica was just getting warmed up when her father interrupted her.

"Jessica, those girls are our guests. They are sweet, shy,. and quiet. It's up to us to make them feel wanted and comfortable in our home." He was wearing his grim don't-talk-back-to-me face.

Jessica was too frustrated and angry to pay attention to any danger signals. "Sweet? Shy? Quiet?" The words came out of Jessica's mouth like bullets. "Those two little jerks are about as quiet as a disco on Saturday night. They did nothing but talk and eat from the time we left this house! Danny spent an absolute fortune on pizza, soda, and popcorn for them. Do you know they can even talk with a faceful of popcorn?" Jessica stormed around the room, picking up pillows, tossing them down, stamping her feet.

"Danny couldn't talk to me. I couldn't talk to him. It was the worst date of my entire life. And do you know whose fault it is? Do you even *care* whose fault it is?"

"Calm down, Jess. You're not making any sense."

Jessica turned on her mother. "Not making

any sense? Nothing makes any sense in this house anymore! Liz is ruining my entire life—and you don't care!"

Jessica regretted the words as soon as they were out of her mouth.

"What has Liz got to do with what happened tonight?"

"What has Liz got to do with it? Well, practically nothing, really. I thought she was going to take care of the twins tonight. I had made plans—important plans. But Liz just took off without a word to me."

"Liz has a right to go out and have a good time," her mother said, "but that does seem thoughtless of her."

Jessica sighed. "It was probably just a mix-up, Mom. And, look, I didn't mean it when I said she was ruining my life."

"We know you didn't, honey," her mother said. "We appreciate how responsibly you acted tonight."

"You know something," Jessica said, looking first at her mother and then at her father. "Responsibility can get in the way of having a good time."

Grinning broadly, Ned Wakefield walked over to her. "I do believe you just discovered one of the great truths of the world," he said, hugging her. "I'm proud of you."

"Thanks, Dad," she said, basking in the glow

of approval and yawning at the same time. "I'm tired. I'll see you in the morning."

As she walked up the stairs, Jessica heard her mother say, "Quite a girl, our Jessica."

The muffled sound of crying hit Jessica's ears as she passed Elizabeth's door. She stopped to listen. She could hear her sister moaning between sobs.

She pushed the door open slowly. "Liz? Hey, Liz, are you OK?" The sobs and moans didn't stop.

Jessica walked over to the bed and sat down on the edge. "Lizzie? It's Jess. What's wrong?"

Elizabeth sat up and wrapped her arms around Jessica's neck tightly. "Oh, Jessie, I'm so glad you're here! I had the most awful nightmare!"

Jessica hugged her sister tightly. "Lizzie, take it easy. Everything's all right."

Elizabeth's arms tightened around Jessica's neck.

"Nightmares don't last forever, Liz," Jessica soothed.

I hope I know what I'm talking about, she added to herself.

Seven

"Is that french toast I smell, Mom?" Jessica asked as she came into the kitchen.

"It's nearly ready, honey. Juice and milk are on the table. Why don't you sit down and get started?"

"It's not fair of you to fix my favorite breakfast."

"Not fair?"

"How am I supposed to fit into my cheerleading outfit, or anything else, if I stuff my face?"

Alice Wakefield smiled as she turned from the stove. "Oh, I think you've got a few pounds to go before people start calling you Tubby. Is Elizabeth on her way down?"

"In a few minutes. She's drying her hair." Jessica flipped open her French book as she sipped her orange juice. "Do you understand irregular verbs, Mom?"

Alice Wakefield appeared lost in thought.

"Mom?"

"Sorry, Jessica. Did you say something?"

"Is anything wrong?"

Alice Wakefield brought her coffee cup over to the table and sat next to Jessica. "I've been wanting to talk to you about Elizabeth."

Jessica felt an overwhelming sense of relief. She and Todd weren't the only ones worried about her twin. She knew her parents were too observant not to have noticed the changes in Elizabeth.

"I've been wanting to talk to you, too, Mom."

Alice Wakefield held up her hand. "Before you say a word, honey, I want you to know that your father and I are aware of what you're going through. You have every right to complain, but you haven't. We're grateful for that, Jess."

"Huh?" What in the world was her mother talking about?

"We've been paying a lot more attention to Elizabeth than to you lately, but I don't want you to think we don't love you every bit as much."

"Mom, I know—"

"Let me finish. I don't want you to resent your sister because of that extra attention."

"Mom, I could never resent Liz!"

"Good. Now, what did you want to say?"

"Oh . . . nothing important, Mom." *Nothing*

except I'm feeling miserable and guilty and worried, she thought.

If her parents hadn't noticed the changes in Elizabeth, how could she tell them?

Elizabeth and Jessica were walking across the front lawn of Sweet Valley High when Jessica spotted Enid Rollins.

"Liz, there's Enid waving at you."

"So?"

"So, if you want to stop and talk to her, I'll see you later."

Elizabeth shrugged irritably. "Enid Rollins is a drag, Jess, and you know it. You always told me to drop her."

Stumped for an answer, Jessica decided it was safer to change the subject. "How's Todd these days? I haven't seen much of him around the house."

"You'd know the answer to that better than I would. I've seen you talking to him often enough, Jess."

Jessica scrambled in her mind for a safe subject. "Ready for today's French test?"

"I plan to have a headache that period," Elizabeth said flatly. "I can always make it up later."

"But, Liz—"

"Don't bug me, Jess. Oh, there's Lila Fowler near the columns. I want to talk to her about tonight's Pi Beta Alpha meeting." Jessica watched her sister dash right past Enid without so much as a nod.

She felt like screaming. Her sister had never cared much about the sorority before. She'd joined only because Jessica had begged and pleaded with her. Now Elizabeth couldn't wait for the next meeting.

"What a joke," Jessica mumbled. "And *I'm* the one who's president of that dumb sorority."

"Who are you talking to, Jess?"

Jessica focused on the figure in front of her. "Oh, hello, Enid."

"Are you all right? You look funny."

"Well, I'm feeling a little funny," she snapped. "What do you want?"

"I want to talk to you about Liz."

"You and the rest of the world," Jessica said, under her breath.

"What?"

"Spit it out, Enid. The first bell's about to ring."

"I was just wondering if Liz has said anything to you about me. It seems like she avoids me at school, and she's never around when I call her. Is she mad at me about something?"

"Not that I know of." Jessica wondered why she didn't tell Enid the truth. Elizabeth didn't want to have anything to do with her. Jessica would have enjoyed telling her to get lost a month ago. For some reason, she felt sympathy for Enid now.

The two girls walked across the lawn in silence for a few moments. As they approached the columns, Jessica said, "I'm sure Liz isn't mad at you, Enid. We're going to the Dairi Burger after school. Why don't you meet us?"

"Hey, thanks, Jess! I'll be there!"

Jessica couldn't understand why she had said that. She certainly didn't care about Enid Rollins's feelings, did she?

If Jessica was enrolled in the "Worrying About Elizabeth" course, Todd was, too. He followed Elizabeth as she hurried under the Romanesque clock and into school. He was close behind when she headed for the bulletin board, and he saw her smile at Ken Matthews. He tried to remember how long it had been since she'd smiled at him in that way. He wished he could hear what they were saying, but with the mob of kids coming into school and going to their lockers, it was impossible.

"Hi, Ken!" said a bubbly Elizabeth.

"Hi, Liz."

"What's new, All-American?"

Ken blushed attractively. "Not much."

"Is that so?" said Elizabeth. "What about the basketball game on Friday? You going?"

Ken looked at her in surprise. "Sure." Everyone knew he never missed a sports event.

"Wish I were going," she said.

"Aren't you?"

"Nobody's asked me," said Elizabeth, her blue-green eyes flashing a seductive glance at him.

"But I thought you always went to see Todd play."

Elizabeth tossed her head and looked annoyed. "That's ancient history."

"Oh," said Ken. He shuffled his feet and looked at the bulletin board and then at the floor.

Elizabeth was still standing very close to Ken when Susan Stewart came down the hall. Practically the whole student body knew that Ken and the pretty redhead had become a twosome lately. Susan spotted them together and walked over quickly.

"Hi, honey," Ken said to Susan as she walked up.

"Hi, Ken," she said, darting a murderous look at Elizabeth.

"Well, see you soon," Elizabeth cooed, then walked off, swaying her hips provocatively. She tried to avoid Todd by turning into the stairwell, but he called to her.

"Liz!"

"Hi, Todd," she said coolly.

"You coming to the game on Friday?"

Elizabeth looked away. "Well, I don't know, Todd. I haven't decided. Listen, I've really got to run. Got to go see Mrs. Green."

"The guidance counselor?" asked Todd.

"Yeah. She's gotten on my case something awful. I've got to tell her to buzz off. See you."

Todd watched her walk away toward Sylvia Green's office and felt more worried than ever.

Mrs. Green watched as Elizabeth came in and sat before her. The guidance counselor was on the alert for signs of change in the former honor student and *Oracle* star reporter. Disturbing reports had been coming in from Elizabeth's teachers.

"Hi," said Elizabeth brightly, looking cheerful.

"Hello, Elizabeth. All recovered, I understand?"

Elizabeth smiled. "I'm better than ever," she said.

"Well," said Mrs. Green. "That's good."

The guidance counselor opened a file before her on her desk and studied it. "I called you in to talk about some of the work you missed."

It was completely unfair, Elizabeth had complained to Jessica. Those crazy teachers actually expected her to make up all the work she'd missed while she was in the hospital, even though it hadn't been her fault she'd been absent. If she did all that homework and those term papers, she'd turn into a drudge. She wouldn't be able to go out at all except on weekends for a month. Out of the question, she had told her sister.

"Yes, ma'am." Elizabeth smiled at the guidance counselor.

"I understand you haven't made up any of the work yet."

"I've been busy."

"I realize that, but I'm afraid you're going to have to make some sacrifices to catch up."

Elizabeth said, "Oh, I know. I'll get to it. I'm just having dizzy spells sometimes."

"Dizzy spells?" Mrs. Green looked at her with concern.

"Yes ma'am. Sometimes I think I'm going to black out."

Mrs. Green studied her. "Maybe you should go back to your doctor?"

"Oh, no," said Elizabeth. "He said I'll be fine. As long as I don't overextend myself. With too many projects." She smiled innocently.

"Well, all right," said Mrs. Green. "It doesn't really matter how soon you do the missed schoolwork. As soon as you feel better. But it must be made up."

"Yes ma'am," Elizabeth said obediently.

Winston Egbert was surprised when Elizabeth slid into a chair beside him in the cafeteria. They had always been friends, especially after he'd taken her to a dance and confessed how crazy he was about Jessica. Of course, Jessica hadn't given him a second glance. Still, Winston had always been grateful to Elizabeth for listening to him that night. But lately, he'd been so busy with Mandy he hadn't talked much to Elizabeth since the accident.

"Hi, Win," she bubbled.

"Hi," he said.

"Before you ask, I'm all better from my vacation in the hospital," said Elizabeth.

"I can see that," said Winston. "I saw you at your pool party."

"I hope I didn't disappoint everybody," she said coquettishly. "I know I looked hopelessly dreadful that night."

"Huh?" said Winston. "Hey, you looked better than Miss America."

"Thanks, you're sweet," she said, picking at a chicken sandwich. "If I were capable of feeling happy, your overly kind words would do it."

"What's the matter?" Winston asked.

Elizabeth sighed deeply.

"Liz?"

"Nothing." A deeper, even more mournful sigh.

"You can tell me, Liz. We're buddies, remember?" Winston Egbert was now a helpless mass of sympathy. "I'd do anything for you, Liz, you know that."

"They expect me to make up hundreds of pages of work I missed and do five hundred term papers, and it makes me so sick I could scream," she said.

"Hey, that's hard."

"If only I didn't have that terrible, long history term paper on the Punic Wars, maybe I could do the rest," said Elizabeth.

"Yeah, that was a tough one," agreed Winston.

"I heard you got an A-plus."

"Yep," said Winston. "Took me two weeks every night. Actually, the wars between Ancient Rome and Carthage are fascinating."

Elizabeth smiled. "I'll bet," she said, and unleashed another painful sigh. "I'm afraid I'll just flunk, that's all."

"Listen, you could do a great paper, Liz. I know you could."

"Sure. If I had the time. But I have so much other work. And I get such horrible headaches. The accident, you know?" A tear rolled down her cheek.

"Listen, I kept a copy of mine."

"Really?"

"If it would help, you could look it over and get my sources. That would cut down on the time."

"Maybe if I just . . . changed it around some?"

"I thought you liked Roman history."

"Oh, I do. But I don't want to have a relapse."

Winston brought Elizabeth his term paper that afternoon in the *Oracle* office. She later turned it in as her own after rewriting a few sentences and paragraphs.

Roger Collins waited until Winston had left, and then he strolled over to Elizabeth's desk. "Hey, Brenda Starr," he said. "Want to talk?"

"Hi, Mr. Collins," she said brightly. "Sure. What's up?"

"Not what's *up*. What's *in*—or *not* in. Such as your 'Eyes and Ears' column for this edition."

"I'm just going to write it."

"OK. How's everything else?"

"Everybody asks me that," she snapped.

"Elizabeth, I hope you know that I'm a friend, not only a teacher and an adviser. And friends don't dish out a lot of applesauce to each other."

"Now what have I done?" Elizabeth asked, sounding hurt.

Mr. Collins let out a breath. "Elizabeth, you know you have to keep your grades up if you want to stay on *The Oracle*. I've been informed you're in danger of failing three courses."

"Well, none of that's fair," said Elizabeth. "I had a little work to make up because of the accident—which wasn't my fault. I needed some time to do it. And I have a term paper I'm just about ready to hand in." She smiled, patting her bag, which held Winston's paper.

"And that's all?" Mr. Collins said.

"I promise you," she said.

"OK, but please remember I'm here if you need help."

"Oh, I'll remember," she said.

Elizabeth turned to writing her column, dropping in little items about who was seeing whom, which romance was flourishing and which one was at its last gasp.

Suddenly she smiled.

"Who is that tall, dark, and handsome stranger Susan Stewart has been dating lately, and does K.M. know about it?" she wrote. "It would be a shame to see this flame flicker out."

"All finished?" Roger Collins said when she handed the column in.

She smiled. "It's finished, all right."

Eight

Todd stalked into the gym for basketball practice feeling frustrated and angry. There was no longer any doubt about it. Elizabeth was through with him. She hardly paid any attention to him, even when he was speaking directly to her, and she was making plays for every guy at Sweet Valley High. They weren't exactly running away from her, either.

OK, then! Who needed Elizabeth Wakefield? *He* did, Todd knew without a doubt. He knew he couldn't blame her for hating him. How could she help but hate him after what he had done to her? He couldn't even blame her if she turned to someone else. But that's what bothered him most. Elizabeth hadn't turned to *some*one else. She had turned to *every*one else, all at the same time. It didn't make sense.

Todd stepped up to the foul line to practice his free throws and missed four in a row. He cursed and bounced the ball roughly into the corner.

Everybody had told Todd how lucky he was to have come out of the motorcycle crash without serious injuries. It was a miracle, Coach Horner said, that his hands hadn't been hurt at all. So after the accident Todd continued to be old reliable at the foul line for the basketball team. "Whizzer" Wilkins they called him, for his sure shooting eye and control under pressure. That's why he was the star of the team.

Nobody noticed anything until the game against Big Mesa, when Todd couldn't hit a basket to save his life.

Elizabeth was there, sitting next to Ken Matthews. Susan Stewart had gotten stuck babysitting for her little brother, so she wasn't there to keep an eye on them. But Todd held an all too watchful gaze, especially when he should have been looking at the basketball.

It was awful. Todd couldn't pass the ball or catch or shoot it.

"Come on, Wilkins," Coach Horner yelled in bewilderment. "Look alive out there."

But it was hopeless. Todd Wilkins, the star of the team, was falling all over his feet like a champion klutz. His eyes were glued on Elizabeth, and after a while even the Big Mesa players noticed it.

On a jump ball in the second half, the Big Mesa center lined up next to Todd and whispered, "Hey, Wilkins, got girl trouble?"

Todd was so shaken he stood there flat-footed while the Big Mesa center grabbed the ball and scored.

"Wilkins," shouted Coach Horner, "are you OK?"

"Sure, coach."

But he wasn't. The game went down the drain in the second half. The Gladiators' whole attack was built around Todd, and when he came apart, so did the team. A strange buzz started after a while, and then it got louder and louder.

Finally, when Todd missed an easy lay-up, the buzzing exploded into a sound he had never heard before while playing at home in the Sweet Valley High gym.

"Booooooo!"

Todd heard it and stopped dead.

"Booooooooo!"

Todd Wilkins was being booed by his own fans. He tried to shake it off, and as he turned to head back up the court, he bumped into the Big Mesa center.

"Boooooooo!" screamed the fans, and the Big Mesa center smiled.

"Hey, Wilkins," he said, laughing, "they're playing your song!"

Todd saw red lights zigzagging in front of him. He saw the laughing Big Mesa player, and suddenly Todd was shoving the hulking center, who was shoving back just as hard. They tussled with each other, almost coming to blows, before the referee came between them.

"You!" he shouted at Todd. "You're out of this game!"

Stunned, Todd trotted back to the Gladiators' bench and sat down with a towel over his head. The boos were louder than ever.

"Sorry, Coach," Todd managed softly.

Coach Horner was a father figure to his boys. Everyone knew how much he cared about them. So after the fateful game against Big Mesa, he sent Todd to an early shower and called the team together. "OK," he said briskly, "what's eating Wilkins?" Coach Horner always sounded tough, but the team knew it was just on the surface. Underneath, he was a softy.

"Elizabeth Wakefield," said Jim Daly.

"Is she his girlfriend or something?"

"Yeah, the twin. The one who got hurt," Jim said.

"She was riding on Todd's motorcycle when it happened, Coach," said Tom Hackett, the guard.

"Uh-huh," said Coach Horner, rubbing his chin. "Is she OK?"

The players all looked away.

"Hey, that was a question! We've got a teammate in trouble here!"

"Todd worries about Liz all the time," said Jim. "She's all he thinks about."

"Why? What's wrong?"

"Coach, Liz Wakefield used to be just about the nicest girl in the whole school. But after that accident, I don't know. She's different."

"I see," said Coach Horner thoughtfully. "I see."

He walked slowly back to his office, where he'd told Todd to wait for him. He opened the door and found his star player hunched miserably in a chair.

"Hello, Todd," he said, sitting down at his desk.

"Hello, Coach."

"Todd, would you like to tell me what happened?" Coach Horner asked with concern.

"I don't know."

"What do you mean you don't know? You almost punched Lane out right in the middle of a game."

"It's all a blur."

"Todd, I believe in giving my players a fair shake, but you've got to help me. What happened?"

Todd shook his head.

"One of the other players said something about a girl," Coach Horner said gently. "Does she have anything to do with this?"

Todd grabbed his head with both hands, trying to keep the coach's words out.

"There are some problems you can't walk away from," Coach Horner said. "Some things just won't let you alone."

"I know, Coach," Todd said softly. Oh, did he know.

"You're going to have to sit out a few games, Todd."

"I know."

"I want you to use that time to get this thing that's troubling you settled. Whatever it is, you can't run away from it."

"Yes, sir."

"From what I hear, Elizabeth's a fine girl. But I think she has problems right now."

Todd Wilkins looked at the coach for the first time. "You think so?"

"Yes, I do, Todd. You acted very out of character, and that's why I knew something was very wrong. If that girl is acting out of character, something's got to be wrong there, too."

Todd smiled weakly as he stood up to leave. He strode down the corridor from the gym. It had been awful, hearing Coach Horner talk about Elizabeth that way. And yet it was a relief. *What an idiot I've been*, he thought. *Of course she's in trouble. That person walking around acting different—that's not my Liz!*

Todd knew he had been a fool not to persist

in getting through to her. Obviously, nobody was doing anything. Everybody had simply accepted the idea that Elizabeth had undergone a permanent personality change. It just couldn't be.

"Something's got to be wrong," Coach Horner had said. Todd knew he had to get to the bottom of it.

Jessica Wakefield was at her wit's end. Everybody treated her like Elizabeth—the old Elizabeth, that is. The responsible one. The one you took your troubles to. The one you went to if you wanted to complain about her sister.

"Listen," Lila Fowler told Jessica in the front corridor, "you tell Elizabeth to keep away from my boyfriend."

"What?" said a not too surprised Jessica.

"Don't act innocent with me," Lila said. "Your dear sister seems to think she can date Tim behind my back. Tell her hands off."

Later, Jessica heard through Cara Walker that Susan Stewart was furious about Elizabeth trying to steal Ken Matthews.

Enid Rollins was just about the last straw. "You know I've always considered Liz to be my best friend."

"Try to understand, Enid—"

"I have tried, Jess, but I've about had it with her," Enid told her. "It was your idea that I meet you at the Dairi Burger. Well, after you left, she made a play for George right under my nose!''

I'm going to have a nervous breakdown, Jessica thought. *All I ever do is worry about Liz.*

And when she wasn't worrying about Elizabeth or trying to find her, she was stuck with all of her sister's work, plus caring for the Percy twins. Things were getting to be a real drag.

One part of Jessica was determined to turn the whole miserable mess over to her parents, but another part of her refused to do that. Her parents hadn't caused the problem, *she* had. She'd gotten Elizabeth into the accident by selfishly leaving Enid's party without her, and worse, she had been the model for Elizabeth's miserable behavior. She was right to keep her worries about Elizabeth from her parents, she was sure. The part of Jessica that was closer to her twin sister than any other person wouldn't let her turn this problem over to anyone else.

Jessica would have been appalled if she could have heard the conversation going on just then between Elizabeth and Roger Collins in the *Oracle* office.

"Elizabeth," said Mr. Collins, "I don't want to believe what I've been told. Is it true that you used your column to try to steal Susan Stewart's boyfriend?"

"What?" asked Elizabeth, her eyes widening into a perfect picture of innocence.

"That's what I've been told," he said. "And here's the item."

He laid the column in front of her. The item about Susan Stewart and "K.M." was outlined in red.

"Why should everybody else have fun because of my column, and not me?" she pouted.

"Then it's true?"

"Well . . . I wrote the item. I really can't help it if Ken Matthews likes me, can I?"

"That's not the point, Elizabeth, and you know it. It's about something called ethics. Something called integrity. You used to understand those words. Not only did you write a self-serving item, but it's not even true. Is it?"

Elizabeth squirmed in her seat.

"Is it true?"

"I don't know every guy Susan runs around with."

"Uh-huh. I thought you and I were never going to dish each other applesauce."

Elizabeth began to cry. "I didn't do anything wrong, Mr. Collins! It's terrible and mean of you to say I did."

"I'm sorry, Elizabeth, truly I am. I hope you can get yourself straightened out. I know you're in trouble with your grades, too."

"I explained that."

"Yes, you did. But until you can explain why you used your column to slander somebody with an item you knew was a lie, I'm afraid I'm going to have to do without you on *The Oracle*."

Elizabeth's eyes widened with surprise. "You're firing me?"

"I'm sorry."

Elizabeth stood up. She glared at him, then tossed her head. "Who cares?" she said. "I thought you were my friend, but I can see I was wrong."

"I am your friend, Elizabeth. You're a fine writer, and I want to help you. I hope whatever is wrong can be cleared up. Until then—"

"Don't hold your breath waiting for me to come back," Elizabeth said haughtily, and sailed out the door.

When Elizabeth got home that afternoon, she saw a white-faced Jessica sitting ramrod straight at the kitchen table with their mother and father, all of them looking as grim as the Supreme Court.

"What's up?" Elizabeth asked.

"Elizabeth, I hardly know what to say to you." Her mother's voice was filled with disappointment. "I never thought a daughter of ours would use another person's term paper and turn it in as her own."

"What?" said Elizabeth, a bright pink flush coloring her face and neck.

"Mrs. Green, your guidance counselor, called

us," her father said. "She's very worried about you."

"We're all worried about you," said Alice Wakefield. Then she turned to Jessica.

"Jessica, why didn't you tell us what was going on? You must have known."

"But I didn't!" Jessica cried. At least not about the paper, she wanted to tell them. And the other stuff . . . well, she hadn't wanted to worry them. She had thought she could handle it on her own, somehow.

Jessica Wakefield felt the world crashing down on her head.

Nine

"Jessica, are you going to drive us to the flute auditions on Saturday?"

The voice startled Jessica. She whirled around, mascara wand in her hand, to see Jean—or was it Joan?—standing in her doorway.

"Did you ever hear of knocking?" she snapped. "It has to do with a little thing called privacy! The whole world has been picking on me, but I thought I was safe in my own room!" She turned back to the mirror.

"You thought you could come in here and make my life miserable, didn't you? You and everyone else in Sweet Valley." Her parents, Todd, and nearly all the girls in school were after her to do something about Elizabeth's behavior, and she had no idea of how to cope with it.

When she looked back toward the doorway, it was empty. *Great,* she thought, *just great.* Now she guessed she was supposed to feel guilty about being nasty to the twin on top of everything else. Jessica felt that if she didn't talk to somebody sympathetic pretty soon, she would fall apart.

After school that afternoon, she stood in the hall outside the *Oracle* office, hoping Mr. Collins wasn't busy. She knew Elizabeth had gone to him with problems in the past, and since this was a problem *about* Elizabeth . . . well, why not?

She pushed the door open and was relieved to see Roger Collins alone in the room. He looked up and smiled at her.

"Liz, I'm glad you stopped by. I felt—"

"Mr. Collins, I'm sorry, but I'm not Liz."

"Jessica? Hey, forgive me. I keep mixing the two of you up these days," he said, moving from his chair to sit on the edge of the desk.

"I'm the one with the worry lines," she said, slumping into a chair.

"And your worries are about your sister, right?"

"Thank goodness you know what I'm talking about, Mr. Collins!" Finally, Jessica felt she had an adult ally. No wonder Elizabeth came to him with problems.

"I can't reinstate her on *The Oracle*, Jessica, not after what she did."

"That's not why I'm here," she said, on the verge of tears.

"Jessica, how can I help?"

"I don't know!" she wailed, unable to hold back the tears. Covering her face with her hands, she began sobbing.

Roger Collins put a comforting arm around Jessica's shoulders, letting her enjoy the release of crying for a few minutes. Then he put a crisp white handkerchief in her hand, patted her shoulder gently, and asked, "Feeling better?"

Sniffling as she dried her tears, Jessica nodded.

"Good. Now tell me what this is all about."

"It's about Liz, what else? Haven't you noticed a difference in her, Mr. Collins?"

Rubbing his chin thoughtfully, the teacher admitted, "Well, her attitude toward *The Oracle* is certainly different."

"See!" She knew she had come to the right person.

"But unfortunately, Jessica, I don't have any solutions. Elizabeth *has* changed, and not for the better, but she doesn't seem to realize it."

Jessica felt as if her last hope had vanished.

"What can we do?" she wailed.

"Right now, I don't know. But at least I'm aware of the problem, and I'll be keeping a close watch on Elizabeth. I know you will be, too. Jessica, be patient. You're Elizabeth's best chance."

Jessica was mulling over her conversation with Mr. Collins when she spotted a long-faced Todd Wilkins sitting on the front steps of the Wakefield house. That could only mean more bad news about Elizabeth.

"What's up, Todd?" she asked, dropping down next to him on the steps.

"Nothing good, Jess. I thought I'd try and talk to Liz, but she's not home, so I decided to hang around and wait." He heaved a big sigh. "Maybe the world will come to an end and put me out of my misery."

Jessica rolled her eyes skyward. "And they say *I* exaggerate! Don't look so down, Todd. Everything's going to work out. It has to," she said, in an effort to cheer him up.

"How, Jess?" he asked in despair.

"We've got to keep cool. I just came from talking to Mr. Collins, and—"

"*You* went to see Mr. Collins?"

"Yes. Why the look of surprise?"

"It just seems so ironic, that's all. I know Liz has gone to him lots of times for advice. He must have been absolutely stunned to find you coming to him."

"Stunned? What do you mean by that, Todd?"

"Well, I mean, he's used to talking to his star reporter, not a . . ." Todd's voice trailed off as he saw the anger on Jessica's face.

"You're implying that a mere cheerleader isn't capable of an intelligent conversation! You're picking on me, and I don't need it, Todd! Everyone is on my case these days. You know, just about none of the girls at school will talk to me without complaining about Liz trying to steal their guys."

She saw Todd wince at that and put her hand on his arm. "I'm sorry, Todd. I shouldn't have said that."

"Why not? It's the truth." He stood, running his fingers through his brown hair in frustration. "I'm probably the only guy in Sweet Valley who leaves Elizabeth cold."

"I'm no better off than you are, Todd. Do you know how many guys come up to me asking me to put in a good word for them with Liz? It's disgusting. They treat me like a buddy— me, Jessica Wakefield, a *buddy!*" Her outrage mingled with Todd's despair as they both paced on the front steps.

"Did you talk to Mr. Collins about Liz and me?" Todd asked.

"No, I didn't," Jessica confessed guiltily. "I guess I was too busy talking about Liz and *me.*"

"It doesn't matter. He may be a wonderful teacher, Jess, but I don't see how he can help."

"I don't know. But he said—"

The end of Jessica's sentence was drowned out by the roar of an approaching motorcycle.

Jessica and Todd turned and saw a bike with two riders coming at them fast. They stood there amazed as Elizabeth zoomed up the Wakefields' driveway and screeched to a halt. She whipped off her helmet, allowing her long blond hair to fall in graceful waves around her face.

"How did I do, Max?" Elizabeth asked as she turned to grin at her passenger, Max Dellon, lead guitarist of Sweet Valley High's favorite rock band, The Droids.

"You are definitely something else, Liz. Like wild, you know? You are the fastest girl biker I've ever seen! Hey, Jess, how about this sister of yours?"

Usually Jessica liked Max. He was a good guitarist and was the perfect image of a rock musician. But at that moment she was furious.

"Girl biker? Elizabeth Wakefield, I'm going to tell Mom and Dad, and they'll send you away to a convent for the rest of your life!" Jessica raged.

"Liz, I've got to talk to you," Todd insisted, taking hold of her arm.

Elizabeth jerked her arm free and stood looking at her sister and Todd.

"You two are *not* being a whole lot of fun."

Jessica opened her mouth to protest, but her twin had already turned away.

"Don't disappear, Max. I'll be right out," Elizabeth said.

Stunned and shaking, Jessica and Todd watched her dash into the house.

Ten

Panic was written all over Jessica's beautiful face as she turned to Todd.

"Todd, you've got to stop her!" Jessica whispered. "You can't let her go out with Max."

"How am I supposed to stop her?" he whispered back. "Besides, Max is a nice person—a little off the wall sometimes, but basically a good guy. Unlike some of your sister's recent dates."

"I don't mean just Max. I mean you can't let her go out with anybody," Jessica insisted.

"Jess, I don't want her going out with other guys, you know that. But I don't own her. I can't tell her who to see." Pain and frustration seemed to be the only emotions left in the world for Todd. It was clear to everyone, including him, that Elizabeth Wakefield was through with him. *Then why do I keep hanging in there?* he asked himself a dozen times a day. The answer was always the same—because he loved her. He loved the *real* Elizabeth, and somehow he had to help her become that person again.

"Todd. Todd, listen to me!" Todd suddenly realized Jessica was pulling on his arm.

"Jess, there's nothing—"

The front door flew open, and Elizabeth, who had changed from jeans to shorts, dashed past Jessica and Todd toward the driveway.

"Elizabeth Wakefield, what do you think you're doing?" Jessica yelled as Elizabeth got on the back of Max's motorcycle. "You know what Mom and Dad said."

"Max and I are just going to the beach for a couple of hours, Jess. Don't get all worked up, for heaven's sake. I'll be back before Mom and Dad get home. 'Bye!"

With a loud vroom, the motorcycle screeched away and went zipping toward the freeway that led to the beach.

"Don't just stand there, Todd, go after them!" Jessica cried frantically.

"I don't have the right, Jess."

"I don't care about *your* rights, Todd Wilkins. All I'm concerned with is *my* head! Mom and Dad have grounded Liz *indefinitely* because of that term paper. I'm supposed to make sure she doesn't go out of the house after school. If they find out she's on a motorcycle, she'll be in more

99

trouble, and I'll probably be grounded, too!" Jessica was on the verge of hysteria. Being a responsible person was getting the best of her.

"I'll do what I can," Todd said, running to his Datsun, which was parked in front of the house. He leaped in and tore away from the curb, heading for the freeway. Ten minutes later he caught up with Elizabeth and Max at a red light. Pulling in front of the motorcycle, Todd strode over to them.

"OK, end of the line," he declared, grabbing Elizabeth's wrist.

"Hey!" she said, trying to jerk free of his grasp.

"Get off that bike!" Todd commanded sternly.

"Let me alone, Todd Wilkins!"

"Hey, Wilkins, ease off," Max said, glancing around.

"Shut up, Max," Todd snapped.

Without further conversation, he forcibly lifted Elizabeth off the motorcycle, carried her over his shoulder to the Datsun, and put her inside, fastening the seat belt securely around her.

"Who do you think you are, pulling a stunt like this?" Elizabeth demanded, furiously.

"Somebody who cares," he said, sliding into the driver's seat.

Todd drove along slowly, trying to look at her as she poured out a torrent of complaints.

"Stop this car right now and let me out! You are kidnapping me! How dare you keep interfering in my life! Haven't I made it absolutely clear that I don't want to be with you?"

Todd drove on. "You've made it clear, all right. I'm just trying to keep you from breaking your neck! I've learned not to ride motorcycles anymore, but it doesn't seem like you have. Why, Liz?"

"It's fun, that's why! Besides, Max Dellon is a *safe* driver," Elizabeth taunted.

Todd flinched at the words but kept driving. They reached the beach, not the swimming area but the dunes farther south. He parked on a bluff overlooking the ocean and turned off the engine.

"Elizabeth," he said, "what's happening?"

"I wish you and everyone else would stop asking me that question. *Nothing* has happened to me," she argued. "I am me, Elizabeth Wakefield, and you'd better take me home right now or—or I'll call the police and tell them you've kidnapped me," she threatened.

"I'll take you home in a few minutes. All I want to do is talk to you, Liz," Todd pleaded.

"Well, *I* don't want to talk to *you*." She slumped down in the seat, a pout marring her lovely features.

"OK. I'll talk, you listen."

Todd sighed, trying to figure out what to say to the girl sitting next to him. He had always known what to say to Elizabeth in the past, but not now. He glanced at her set profile and knew she wasn't going to make this easy for him.

"Liz, I just don't understand what's going on," he began.

She turned her face away so he couldn't even see her profile.

"It's not like you to get behind in your schoolwork—or to cheat on a term paper! Jess told me you were grounded, yet you went out anyway. Don't you care what your parents or any of your old friends think?"

Elizabeth maintained a hostile silence.

Her reaction was unnerving him, but Todd continued. "And that was a dirty trick you played on Susan Stewart and Ken Matthews with the phony item in your column."

Still she didn't answer. Todd had just about run out of arguments.

"How about what you're doing to your sister? Jess cares about you, Liz. She doesn't deserve the kind of treatment you're handing out."

This time Todd had struck a nerve. Elizabeth snapped her head around to face him with a triumphant smile. "That's it! That's what this is all about. You're worried about Jess, aren't you? And here I thought you didn't even like her. Well, that's fine with me. You two would make a lovely couple. Both of you are born worriers," she said. "Take me home *now*."

Muttering under his breath, Todd started the car and drove back to Sweet Valley. At the Wakefield house, Elizabeth got out of the car and hurried up the brick walk just as an anxious Jessica opened the door.

"Oh, Liz, I'm so glad you're home!"

"I'm tired, Jess. I'm going up to my room to sleep." Elizabeth walked into the house, seemingly unaware of the concerned look on her sister's face.

"Don't worry about Mom and Dad, Lizzie," Jessica called after her. "I won't tell them a thing, I promise." Then she turned back to Todd. "Thanks."

"Yeah."

"Did you have any luck talking to her?" she asked hopefully, although she already knew the answer. His expression was even glummer than before.

"Sure I had luck," he said. "All of it bad. I talked, she *didn't* listen. I just don't know what else to do, Jess."

They stood there lost in thought, each trying to think of a way to help Elizabeth.

"I've got it," Jessica said brightly. "We'll talk to Mr. Collins again!"

"Do you think it'll do any good?"

"Or maybe we could find that gorgeous hunk of a psychology professor who spoke at assembly last week."

"Are you interested in advice or the gorgeous hunk?"

"With the way my life is going these days, if I got someone like him interested in me, Liz would just come along, smile, bat her eyelashes at him, and take him away from me."

Todd looked at her in amazement. She jabbed him lightly in the ribs with her elbow. "That's called laughing through the pain, Todd. I think it's what you and I are supposed to do at a time like this."

Todd grinned at this suddenly down-to-earth Jessica. "You know, Jess, you surprise me. Maybe you and I could become—"

"If you dare ask me to be your buddy, Todd Wilkins, I'll slug you, I really will!"

Later that night, Alice and Ned Wakefield were in the kitchen planning the next day's activities. Jessica had gone to bed early with a headache.

"There's just no way I can change my morning appointment, Ned. Can you rearrange your schedule?"

"Can't do it, Alice," he said, shaking his head. "I have to be in Claremont by nine for that hearing in district court. That means leaving here no later than seven."

"Well, someone has to drive Jean and Joan to

that audition. Liz is grounded, so I guess it's up to Jessica. What do you think?"

"There have been some big changes in Jessica lately," Ned Wakefield said proudly. "I'm sure she can handle it."

Eleven

"Jessica, it's time. Can you hear me, Jessica?"

Jessica gave no sign of understanding the small, tentative voice.

"Jessica, your mother said we should wake you."

In some distant corner of her mind, Jessica was aware of voices disturbing her sleep. She burrowed her head further under the pillow, hoping the voices would stop.

Jean and Joan Percy stood there looking down at the inert body on the bed.

"What should we do?" Jean whispered.

"Maybe we should shake her a little," Joan suggested.

The girls stared at each other, wide-eyed. They had been in the Wakefield house long enough to know they should steer clear of Jessica when she first woke up.

Jessica, realizing that the source of the voices was still present, mumbled something unintelligible. Jean and Joan moved quickly away from the bed. If the sleeping monster was going to waken, they did not want to be within arm's reach.

Almost as if she could feel two intense, dark gazes boring into her, Jessica stirred. She opened one eye, saw the twins, and quickly shut it. "It has to be a nightmare. I have to be dreaming," Jessica muttered. "If they're still there when I open my eye again, I'll *kill* them," she vowed.

"Jessica, your mother says it's time to get up, honest," Jean said.

"She's right," Joan said.

"You are both lying!" Jessica wasn't muttering any longer. She was wide awake, sitting up and glaring at the girls. "My mother loves me. There is no way she would want me to get up in the middle of the night!"

"It's seven o'clock, and if we don't hurry, we'll be late."

"There is absolutely nothing in the world you can be late for at this unreal hour," Jessica snapped. "Even the queen of England didn't have to get up this early for her own coronation."

She sat on her bed cross-legged, trying to rub the sleep out of her eyes.

"Your mother said you would drive us to the flute auditions," Jean said quietly.

"What?"

"We have to be there at eight-thirty, and the school is kind of far away. *Please,* Jessica," Joan implored, overcoming her fright. Fear took second place when playing the flute was involved.

"Well, that's just too bad, because I'm not doing it," Jessica said flatly. "I have my day all planned, and it definitely does not include driving you two to some dumb audition."

When the twins remained standing and staring at her, Jessica gave up the thought of going back to sleep.

"Don't look at me like that. I told you I have plans. Danny Stauffer invited me to go to the beach this afternoon. I think he's finally forgiven me for that disastrous time at the drive-in. You remember that night, don't you? Now you expect me to blow another date with him to take you someplace? No way!"

"Your mother said—"

"My mother is going to change her mind," Jessica interrupted. She got up and started for the door. "I'll talk to her right now."

Before she could get out of the room, Joan blurted, "Your mother left a few minutes ago. She had to drive your father someplace. She left this note for you."

Jessica took the paper from her. She read it and knew her day was going to be ruined:

Dear Jess,

You were asleep last night when your father and I realized we both had appointments this morning. Joan and Jean have their auditions this morning, too. Could you please take them? Your dad and I really appreciate it.

Love you,
Mom

"This is her idea of *love*?" Jessica said, not expecting an answer from the Percy sisters.

Jessica heaved a disgusted sigh. She had no choice but to do what her mother asked her.

"OK, OK. Where is this place and how long does one of these stupid things take?" she snarled.

When the twins told her where the auditions were being held and that each one took only about five or ten minutes, Jessica's spirits soared. She could do her chauffeuring routine and have plenty of time to meet Danny at the beach, she thought. It should be easy—if she didn't pay too much attention to speed limits.

"That's the place, Jessica! See the sign?" Jean shouted. "Look at all those cars."

Jessica looked at the crowded grammar school parking lot and groaned. It had taken almost an hour to get there because of the heavy Saturday traffic. No one *she* knew ever got on the freeway so early in the morning.

"Look, you two, I'll let you out in front. You go in and do your thing, then come on out to the lot. I'll be looking for you." She checked the time on the dashboard clock, wishing for once in her life that she had a wristwatch. Time had never seemed so important before. "It should take twenty, maybe thirty minutes, right?"

Four very frightened brown eyes looked at her.

"What *is* the matter?" she asked impatiently.

Jean and Joan looked at each other, then at Jessica.

"Aren't you coming in with us?" Jean asked.

"Mom *always* comes in with us," Joan added.

"I am *not* your mother!"

"But you're kind of like a big sister, aren't you, Jessica? Please. We can't go in there *alone*."

Jessica looked from one terrified face to the other. How had she gotten herself into this mess? It didn't take long to find the answer. Elizabeth. She knew the old Elizabeth would be kind and understanding and supportive in this kind of situation. Jessica wasn't sure if she could be any of those things, but she was there, and she was stuck with it.

"OK, you little munchkins, out! I'll park the car and meet you in the lobby," she said, resigning herself to the chore.

The twins scrambled out of the car, black flute cases under their arms, and joined the stream of young musicians entering the building.

Jessica stomped down hard on the accelerator, tearing around the lot until she found an empty space.

She was appalled at the crowd in the front lobby of the grammar school. *Terrific*, she said to herself. A mob of pushy parents and a zillion scared little rabbits. This was one strange place for Jessica Wakefield.

She had no sooner gotten inside when Jean and Joan surrounded her. "OK, kids," she said, "let's get the show on the road."

"Will you go up to the desk and tell the woman who we are?" Jean asked timidly.

"You want me to go up and tell her you are a large pain in the butt?" Jessica snapped.

Those eyes were focused on her again.

"Come on. Let's get this whole disaster over," Jessica said as she dragged them to the long registration table.

"Can I help you?" a woman asked.

"I doubt it, but it's worth a try," Jessica muttered.

"I beg your pardon, miss?"

"These two kids are here to audition." Jessica pulled the two girls closer to the table.

"More flute players, I see," the woman said as she glanced at their leather cases.

"Yes. Can they audition right now, please?

111

We have a long way to drive home and a *very* important appointment at noon." Jessica put on her most sincere smile, the one that was so effective at getting her what she wanted from adults.

The woman smiled back. It was working!

"Let's see what we can do, dear. A number of players have already registered this morning, so your sisters will have to wait their turns." She glanced down at a list on the table.

Jessica didn't bother to correct the woman, but she decided she must need glasses if she saw any resemblance between these two brown wrens and a dazzling blonde like herself.

"All right, girls, sign your names on the bottom of this list. Your audition numbers are seventy-two and seventy-three."

"Seventy-two and seventy-three!" Jessica gasped. "That can't be!"

Jessica thought she had never been more annoyed in her life. But she was wrong. True annoyance came after she had spent five hours restlessly pacing the musty corridors of the school, listening to interminable noises from flutes, trumpets, trombones, and heaven only knew what. Finally the twins' numbers were called. They disappeared into a room and emerged a short time later.

"I think I made it," Jean said gleefully.

"I bombed out," Joan said.

"What was all that terrible stuff you were playing?" Jessica asked.

"Terrible? That was a Bach sonata."

"Are you two through now? Can we go?"

"Sure," Joan said. "It was really great of you to bring us."

Jessica hardly listened. She herded them to the car and took off toward Sweet Valley in a fever.

She thought at first it was just the echo of all that flute playing in her ear, until she saw the flashing lights in the rearview mirror.

Jessica pounded the steering wheel with the flat of her hand. She was being frustrated on every side.

"License and registration, miss," the trooper said.

This was definitely the spot to use a for-adults-only smile, and Jessica gave it everything she had.

"Oh, officer, I'm so sorry. Was I going just a little bit over the speed limit?" One large tear miraculously appeared in her right eye.

"Fifteen miles is more than just a little bit, young lady," the trooper said, totally unmoved by the threat of tears. "You were endangering your life and the lives of others. And you put your little sisters in jeopardy," he added.

That did it!

"These are not my sisters, as anyone with half an eye could tell," she said with an edge to

113

her words. "If you'll just give me that ticket, I'll be on my way." *If I hurry*, she thought, *maybe I can still catch Danny at the beach.*

"Jessica, that policeman told you not to drive so fast," Jean complained as the little red car hurtled along the way to the beach.

"Well, if you had learned to play the flute faster, I wouldn't have to drive so fast. Just keep quiet and let me concentrate on the road!"

She swung the car sharply into an empty parking space and jumped out, followed by the twins.

"Are we going to go swimming, Jessica?" Joan asked.

"No, we are not going to go swimming," Jessica answered angrily.

She scanned the beach crowd, hoping for a glimpse of Danny. He just had to be there.

"There he is, Jessica."

"Where? Where?"

"Over there with his arm around that pretty girl in the white bikini." Jean pointed him out.

"The nerve of him! Just because I was a few hours late, he picks up someone else," Jessica fumed. "Let's go," she said to the girls and stomped back to the car in disgust. "I refuse to waste another minute of my time on that jerk."

They quickly got into the car, and as Jessica was backing out, she said angrily, "Don't you ever, *ever* ask me to take you anyplace again! Is that clear?" She had her eyes on them, and as a result, Jessica Wakefield and disaster collided once more.

The crunch of fenders was the worst sound Jessica had ever heard. She jammed on the brakes and did the only thing possible. She put her arms on the steering wheel, buried her face in her hands, and cried.

Twelve

Most of the kids at Sweet Valley High considered Lila Fowler just about the biggest snob around, but they had to hand it to her when it came to having a party. When the Fowlers threw open their sprawling estate on the hill, they went all out. There were lights around the Spanish courtyard, and the hottest band in Southern California played by the swimming pool.

Lila never gave a party without a theme, and this time she had combined two of her old favorites. The kids were told to come in costume and without a date to a "pickup party." Everybody came single and picked up whomever they could. A lot of girls at Sweet Valley who thought they were going steady found themselves without boyfriends after one of Lila's pickup bashes, and a lot of girls who wanted to get rid of guys did so that same night. Jessica liked the idea because it would give her a chance at just about every neat guy there.

It had taken the Wakefield twins almost an hour of heroic promises to get permission to go to the party.

"Elizabeth is grounded," Alice Wakefield had said. "No dates."

"But, Mom, there won't *be* dates. Everybody's going single. We'll be together," Jessica argued.

"Oh, please," Elizabeth had chimed in. "I'll do all my homework, really! And I haven't felt this good in so long."

It was a losing battle for Alice Wakefield when both her twin daughters overwhelmed her with appeals at the same time.

"Well, all right," she had said finally. "But, Jessica, you take care of your sister."

"I will," Jessica had said and sighed.

The beautiful twins were both dressed as matadors, but with different-colored accessories. Elizabeth's were red, and Jessica's were green. As usual when they dressed nearly the same, they succeeded in fooling most of the kids for a while.

But pretty soon the twin with the red sash and jacket was flirting so outrageously with every boy present that everyone knew it was Elizabeth.

"Boy, your sister is going all out tonight," Lila said as the red twin twirled through a group of boys near the band. "But I really do wish you would put a lid on her." Lila sighed. "It's becoming an absolute bore, you know."

"Lila, that *is* my sister you're talking about. Knock it off!" Jessica said angrily.

Jessica felt rotten about blowing up at Lila, but she didn't have time to apologize. She had to keep an eye on Elizabeth.

The flirtatious twin in the red-trimmed matador suit was having a wonderful time, while the one in green stood on the sidelines.

"Hey, Jess, are you just going to stand around all evening watching your sister?" Cara Walker asked.

"I *have* to watch her." Jessica said dejectedly. "I promised my mother."

Under the lanterns Elizabeth spun madly across the red Spanish tiles. The world about her became a spinning blur. Suddenly she whirled into the arms of another boy. He was tall and strong, and when she looked at his face, she saw it was Todd.

"Liz," he said.

"No, thanks, Todd." She turned away.

The music erupted into a driving, powerful beat, and Elizabeth spun once more, moving happily and swiftly, smiling at each boy she passed. Once again, she was in somebody's arms.

"Hello, Jessica," Bruce Patman said.

Elizabeth didn't say a word, she just gave Bruce a flirtatious smile.

Tall, dark-haired Bruce was easily the best-looking guy at Sweet Valley High, and the richest. He was well aware that with his looks, his father's money, and his fantastic talent on the tennis courts, he could date any girl in town—except either of the Wakefield twins. Sometime back he'd done a real number on Jessica, and he figured that pretty much finished him with either Wakefield.

He didn't understand why Jessica was flirting with him now, but he was going to make the most of it. "You're looking sensational, Jess," he said.

Elizabeth's face glowed with excitement. Bruce's arms were around her, and they moved rhythmically to the beat. They danced under the lanterns and behind the palm trees, where Bruce nuzzled her neck and tried to kiss her. She laughed and moved them back out onto the patio.

"You're in a teasing mood tonight, Jessica," he said.

"Really?"

"Really. But don't stop. You seem different. I don't think I've ever realized just how terrific you are."

Elizabeth laughed wildly.

Whirling past the band, Bruce spotted Max

Dellon lounging against the bandstand watching them, grinning knowingly.

"What's so funny?" Bruce asked.

"You and Liz," said Max. "I didn't know you were an item. But then, this is pickup night."

Bruce examined the face of his lovely partner. It was beautiful, all right. He had thought it was Jessica. Now he remembered he'd heard Elizabeth was going through a mysterious illness and wasn't acting like herself.

"You aren't Jessica," he said. "You're Elizabeth."

Elizabeth laughed. "Fooled you."

She made no attempt to pull away from him, though. She seemed quite content in his arms.

"You like me?" he asked, probing her situation.

She smiled. "Why shouldn't I?"

"Just wondering. You know who I am?"

"Sure," Elizabeth giggled. "Bruce Patman."

Now Bruce smiled. Elizabeth Wakefield, the beautiful girl who had snubbed him a thousand times, who thought she was too good for him, was in his arms at last.

"I thought you were Jessica at first," he said.

Elizabeth tossed her head. "Really? Don't you think I'm just as exciting as Jessica?"

Bruce looked into her eyes. Was she putting him on? "You like excitement?"

"Of course. Who doesn't?"

"Want a drink?"

"Sure! What do you have?"

Bruce led her back behind a palm tree and pulled a small bottle from his pocket. He took the cap off and, still doubtful, handed it to her. But Elizabeth grabbed the bottle and gulped down several quick slugs. Bruce had to grab it back. "Hey, take it easy."

Elizabeth laughed and ran back out onto the dance floor, just in time to meet Jessica, who'd been searching anxiously for her.

"Liz," she said, "are you all right?"

" 'Course," said Elizabeth, her eyes wide.

"OK. I'm going to dance a little. I'll see you later. Take it easy, will you?"

"See you," said Elizabeth.

Bruce watched from behind the palms. When Jessica was gone, he stepped out and took Elizabeth's hand. With a little tug, he pulled her back into the shadows. Elizabeth didn't resist. Instead, she gave him another dazzling smile.

Well, well, well, thought Bruce. *So you're in my power, huh?*

Bruce kissed her. Then again, harder. Elizabeth responded by throwing her arms around his neck.

"You're wonderful, Liz," Bruce murmured.

The music slowed down, and the lights grew dim as the evening progressed. Elizabeth danced steadily with Bruce Patman, her head comfortably on his chest.

When Jessica realized it, she managed to pry

Elizabeth away for a moment. "Liz," she whispered.

"Hmmm?"

"Liz, you know you're dancing with Bruce Patman?"

"Isn't he wonderful?" Elizabeth murmured.

"Wonderful? *Bruce Patman?*"

"Yes. I'm very interested in him."

"But you hate him, Lizzie."

"Who told you that?"

"You did, a hundred and thirty-seven times."

"Silly," said Elizabeth. "Go away."

Jessica kept her eye on Elizabeth and Bruce after that as they kept dancing cheek to cheek under the palms. She couldn't believe it. Jessica might be able to handle that obnoxious, pushy creep, but could her unpredictable sister?

"What's the matter?" Lila Fowler asked later, when she saw Jessica frowning.

"My sister and Bruce," Jessica said.

"They seem to be a new item," said Lila. "My pickup parties surprise even me sometimes."

"Well, he seems to be behaving himself," Jessica said. "So far."

It was another of those impossible evenings for Jessica, when she found her own fun utterly destroyed by having to worry about her sister. Was this what used to happen to Elizabeth? Had Jessica run around irresponsibly so that Elizabeth was forever watching out for her? Jessica vowed that if her sister ever returned to her sweet old self, she'd never give her cause to worry again.

Bruce Patman was becoming more and more intrigued as the evening wore on. He'd kissed Elizabeth—and not only hadn't she pushed him away, she'd responded. Enthusiastically.

"I didn't think you liked me," he said.

"Why shouldn't I?" purred Elizabeth.

"No reason. But you always used to be stuck-up and afraid to do anything."

"That's not me."

"What would you like to do?"

"Anything you want."

"Really?"

"Sure, Bruce, honey."

Bruce laughed with abandon. Elizabeth laughed with him.

"This is going to be some kind of night, Liz," he said.

"I hope so," she said.

"You want to go to my dad's club with me?"

"Sure."

"It's down on the beach," he said.

"I don't care if it's on the moon," Elizabeth said recklessly.

A little while later Jessica looked around and could find no trace of her sister. Bruce Patman was gone, too. *Uh-oh*, she thought, and made the rounds of the Fowler house looking for them.

There was no sign of them on the dance floor, at the buffet table in the dining room, or around the bandstand. She checked the cars parked around the curving front drive but found only other couples who didn't appreciate being disturbed.

Finally she ran to Lila. "Have you seen Liz?"

"She's with Bruce."

"But I can't find them, Lila."

"Oh, I think they left, Jess. They went to Bruce's father's club with some of the kids."

"Oh, no," said Jessica. She looked around anxiously, wondering what to do. Then her eyes fell upon the only one she could trust.

"Todd, it's Liz and Bruce. They've left together."

Todd didn't have to be told another word.

"Where?" he asked sharply.

"I think to Bruce's father's club—down on the beach."

"OK," he said, and ran to his car.

Bruce Patman's sleek black Porsche moved swiftly through the night. Elizabeth had glued herself to his side. He couldn't believe it. She was really his for the taking.

He parked the Porsche carefully under the redwood overhang on the beach side of the Driftwood Club, and Elizabeth reached for the handle of the door.

"Don't, baby," Bruce whispered, pulling her hand away from the door.

"But, Bruce, the other kids are already going in," she said, glancing out the window. "We don't want to miss any of the party, do we?" she asked, her voice showing the effect of the liquor Bruce had given her at Lila's.

"We could have our own party, just the two of us," he suggested in a husky voice.

"But I want some wine." She giggled. "Wine makes me feel soooooo good." She snuggled against him.

"I've got enough wine right here in the car to make you feel *very* good, sweet Liz." He pulled her closer, kissing her on her slender, vulnerable neck.

"Oh, I like that! Sweet Liz, that's me!" She giggled again. "And I like whatever it is you're doing to my neck."

For the twentieth time that night, Bruce Patman wondered how he had gotten so lucky. Elizabeth Wakefield was about to melt in his arms. It would take just a little more to drink and just a little more time.

"As soon as the gang gets into the club, I'll take care of more than your neck," he promised. "Have some wine, my sweet Liz." He reached behind his seat and pulled out an already opened bottle, as well as a paper cup. Filling the cup, he handed it to her, then took a swig from the bottle.

He kept his arm around Elizabeth as she greedily drank down the warm wine. "I've got a blanket in the trunk," he whispered into her ear. "We'll take the wine and the blanket and go down to the beach and—"

The door on the driver's side was suddenly jerked open, and Bruce felt a hard hand on his arm dragging him away from Elizabeth and out of the car. The bottle of wine fell to the ground and shattered.

"What the—" was all Bruce got out before he felt a fist on his jaw. The blow left him out cold on the driveway.

"What are you doing, Bruce?" Elizabeth's speech was slurred, and she tried to focus her eyes on the dim form that was looking down at her. "What happened to our party?"

"The party's over, Liz. I'm taking you home." Todd pulled her gently from the Porsche and guided her to his beat-up car. She was so unsteady on her feet that Todd was almost carrying her. Todd settled her in the car, buckled the safety belt around her, and got into the driver's seat. He had just started the car when Elizabeth sat up straight, recognizing him at last.

"You know, Todd, you're getting to be a real party pooper," she slurred just before she passed out.

Thirteen

"Stay right where you are, young lady," Alice Wakefield said in a tone Jessica was very familiar with.

"Don't you want me to clear the table?" Jessica asked hopefully. She didn't think she was going to escape the coming lecture, but it was worth a try.

"Sit down, Jessica," Ned Wakefield said sternly.

Jessica knew she was really in for it if her father was going to get involved in the discussion.

"First, Jessica, suppose you tell us why you didn't inform us of the speeding ticket and the dent in the car when you got home on Saturday," her mother said.

Jessica shifted uncomfortably in her chair. She knew why she hadn't told them. They would

127

have started yelling and lecturing, but she could have handled that. The real reason for her silence was the grounding she knew would come. She hadn't wanted to miss Lila's party. And it was a darn good thing she *had* been there. Who knew what would have happened between Elizabeth and Bruce if she hadn't sent Todd after them? She'd been very responsible that night, and where had it gotten her—in trouble again. It just wasn't fair!

"I was going to tell you about it sooner, really I was," Jessica began in her own defense. "But I—"

"But what?"

"Well, I know you have so many things on your minds these days, and I just didn't want to add to your worries." She didn't really think they would buy that, but it couldn't hurt to try.

"Your consideration for our feelings overwhelms me, Jessica," her father said dryly.

"Oh, all right! I didn't tell you because I knew you wouldn't see my side of it. I *knew* you would ground me. Why don't you pass judgment and sentence me without going through the motions of a hearing?" Jessica said, somewhere between tears and anger.

"Jessica, you can't expect us to ignore the reckless and irresponsible way you were driving," Alice said.

"But it wasn't as bad as it looks, honest! I wasn't going all that fast, and the dent wasn't really my fault," she pleaded, looking from one parent to the other.

"Seventy miles an hour isn't all that fast?" her father queried, arching one eyebrow.

"Excuse me, Mr. Wakefield."

The three Wakefields turned toward the doorway of the kitchen and saw Jean and Joan looking at them.

"What is it, girls?" Ned Wakefield asked.

"Could we talk to you for a minute?"

"Can it wait until we finish talking to Jessica?"

"That's what we wanted to talk to you about," Joan said.

Just what I need, Jessica thought. *With those two on the witness stand, I'll probably get sent to the electric chair.*

"OK, come in, girls. You were with Jessica that day. Maybe you can tell us what happened."

"Jessica couldn't have been going as fast as the policeman said she was," Jean stated. "It's not possible."

Mr. Wakefield smiled at them. "I know you want to help Jess, but she was tracked by radar. She *was* doing seventy."

"She couldn't have been, Mr. Wakefield. Those radar guns sometimes make mistakes. My dad told me that once a big old oak tree was clocked at forty miles an hour."

"And besides that," Joan put in, "I always get carsick at high speeds, and I felt just fine that day."

129

Jessica blinked in astonishment. They were defending her. They were actually on *her* side.

"And about that dent," Joan continued. "Jessica started backing out first. That man in the other car was more to blame than she was."

"It looks like you have a couple of pretty good defense attorneys," Ned Wakefield said, smiling. "What do you think, Alice?"

"I think you and I may have overreacted, Ned," she answered. "Perhaps this was a case of carelessness, not recklessness." She turned to Jessica, catching the look of total relief. "But don't think you're off the hook entirely, young lady. There will be a punishment. Your father and I will discuss this further and talk to you about it later."

Jessica smiled happily. She could hardly believe her good luck. "Thanks, Mom and Dad. Thanks so much! You have my solemn promise that I'll never go even a half mile over the speed limit again!" She threw her arms around her mother, hugging her tightly.

Alice Wakefield found it impossible not to laugh along with her daughter. Disentangling herself, she suggested, "Don't you think you should save some of the thanks for your two friends?" She nodded in the direction of Joan and Jean as she and Mr. Wakefield left the room.

Jessica eyed the two girls for a moment. What in the world was she supposed to say to them?

The twins exchanged glances and then looked at Jessica.

"We're sorry we were so much trouble for you, Jessica," said Joan.

"Trouble?"

"Well, you know, the night of the drive-in and then again with the auditions."

"Well, I'm sorry I yelled at you so much," Jessica said.

"Oh, that's all right," Joan said.

"We get yelled at lots more sometimes. That was nothing."

"Really? Your parents yell at you?"

"Oh, no," said Joan.

"Never," added Jean.

"It's Mr. Minor, our flute teacher. Boy, he's nuclear!" They both giggled.

"Besides, we never had so much fun," said Joan.

"Never," Jean said. "Boy, going to a real drive-in! With making out and everything."

"Wait a minute," Jessica said.

"Nobody ever takes us places like *that*," said Joan. "Wait till we tell the kids."

"Listen, you two," Jessica said, "cool it, see? You weren't supposed to be there." But she looked at their solemn little faces and couldn't help laughing.

As Jean and Joan left the room, the closeness between them was obvious. It made Jessica want to cry. She and Elizabeth had been like that, sharing everything, protecting and sticking up for one another. But not anymore. And she missed that closeness. Losing out on dates, having her parents angry at her—none of that was important. She needed Elizabeth, her sister . . . her friend.

"Hey, Liz! Wait up!"

Elizabeth turned around and saw Bill Chase coming down the corridor toward her. He was wearing his usual land outfit of jeans and a T-shirt. His long, straight blond hair was dry for a change, and he was carrying books instead of a surfboard.

"How's the surf these days?" she asked, smiling up at him in a flirty way that took him by surprise.

"Terrific—as usual."

Since he was only truly alive when he surfed or gave surfing lessons, Bill didn't spend much time hanging out with the kids at school. But Todd Wilkins was a good friend of his, so he did know that Todd and Elizabeth were not going together any longer.

Bill remembered how surprised he'd been when Todd told him how cold Elizabeth was being.

"Is it really all over?" he had asked. "What happened?"

"It's over, Bill," Todd had said sadly. "But I'd rather not talk about it."

"I'm not trying to pry, Todd, and I really feel bad for you. Sounds like Elizabeth is acting rotten."

Todd sighed. "No, Bill. But she seems mixed up. If she'd find someone else who's special, that would be one thing. But she just doesn't act like she knows what she's doing."

"Todd, you're really worried about her."

"Yes, I am."

"You know I've always cared about Liz."

"I know."

"I mean, if it's really over between you two, I was wondering if you'd get mad at me if I asked Liz out."

Todd turned away, and Bill thought at first he was really angry. But then Todd sighed again and looked back. The expression on his face wasn't anger. It was worry and sorrow.

"It isn't up to me who she goes out with," he murmured.

"I know, but I don't want you mad at me."

Todd looked down at his shoes. "Don't worry about it, Bill. I won't mind if you ask her out. I haven't got the right. I'll see you later."

Bill hadn't needed any more urging. He had been half in love with Elizabeth from a distance for ages.

"I was wondering if maybe you'd like to go

to the beach club dance with me Saturday night," he asked Elizabeth hesitantly.

"Beach club? Hmmmm . . ."

"If you've got other plans, it's OK. I didn't really expect you to be free."

"Why not? Sure, I'll go—on one condition," she said, surprising him. "I'll go if you'll take me surfing the next day."

"I've never seen you do much surfing," he said, confused. Afraid that she might change her mind about Saturday night, he quickly added, "Sure, I'll take you surfing."

"Can I go way out, Bill, where you go?" Elizabeth's smile was almost hypnotizing him.

Bill blinked in surprise. "That's kind of dangerous for an inexperienced surfer," he warned.

"But I wouldn't be in any danger with you along to protect me, would I, Bill?"

Bill Chase suddenly knew what it meant to be able to leap tall buildings in a single bound.

"I'd always take care of you, Liz."

"See you Saturday night, then."

Bill stared after her in amazement as she walked sexily down the hall.

He would also have been amazed to hear her on the phone with Bruce Patman later that day.

"Hi, baby, how are you?" Bruce asked.

"I'm just terrific, Bruce. How's your glass jaw?" She laughed.

"You little wildcat. You like the idea of two guys fighting over you, don't you?" he accused.

"Well, Bruce, it was kind of fun, but I wish you'd been the winner."

"Yeah? Well, how about proving it Saturday night? My folks are away for the weekend, and we could go to the beach house. We'd have it all to ourselves, just you and me together, the whole night through. What do you say, sweet Liz?" Bruce kept his voice low and sexy.

Elizabeth didn't even hesitate before saying, "You've got a date, Bruce. But don't pick me up here. My folks are a little square when it comes to certain things. I'll meet you around the corner from my house."

A nervous Bill Chase rang the Wakefields' bell that Saturday night. He was still surprised that Elizabeth had agreed to go out with him.

"Bill Chase, what are you doing here?" Jessica asked as she opened the door.

"Hello, Jess. I'm here to pick up Liz. Is she ready?"

"Liz? Uh—come in."

She led Bill into the living room and told him to wait, trying frantically to think of a way of covering for her absent sister.

"I'll be right back," she said, dashing up the stairs.

"Oh, boy, oh, boy, oh, boy!" she muttered as she dialed Enid Rollins's number. Elizabeth had said she was spending the night there, obviously forgetting she had a date. When did those two become friends again? Jessica wondered.

"Enid, it's Jess, let me speak to Liz," she snapped, in no mood to be polite. She listened for a moment, then banged down the phone.

"Great! She's not there," Jessica muttered to herself. "That could only mean she's out with someone else—someone she shouldn't be with. Talk about fast lanes! I'd better give Bill the bad news." She started out of her room, then stopped when an idea hit her.

Why should Liz have all the fun? she asked herself.

Five minutes later she surveyed the transformation. She was wearing Elizabeth's flowered peasant skirt and ruffled blouse. She strolled down the stairs and into the living room.

"I'm sorry to keep you waiting, Bill."

He smiled. "You're worth waiting for, Liz."

At the same time that Bill was driving off with the Wakefield twin he thought was Elizabeth, Bruce and the real Elizabeth arrived at the Patmans' luxurious beach house. Bruce led her from the car around to the pool in the back of the house.

"Nice, Bruce, *very* nice." Elizabeth looked around at the beautifully landscaped deck area, the lounge chairs arranged near the pool, the glass-topped table, the subdued lighting. It was a California dream house.

"How about a swim?" Bruce suggested.

"I didn't bring my suit," she replied.

"Who needs a suit?" Bruce grinned suggestively.

"First things first, Bruce," she said. "Show me around this gorgeous place."

"You're right. We'll cool off later. Much later." He pulled her down onto a lounge chair and into his arms for a long, probing kiss.

"This is the pool deck," he whispered between kisses.

Fourteen

"Bruce!" Elizabeth protested laughingly, breaking free of him.

"Hey, what's the matter? I thought you liked me. You certainly liked me the other night." Bruce's handsome face was flushed with anger. Girls did not usually play hard to get with him.

"Bruce, you're even better looking when you're mad," Elizabeth teased. "You know I wouldn't be here tonight if I didn't like you—and your kisses, too." She put a hand on his arm and smiled up at him. "I just don't like to be rushed, OK?"

Bruce shrugged and stood up. "All right, Liz. I won't rush you, but don't keep me waiting too long," he warned.

"I won't, Bruce," she promised.

Tugging on her hand, he whispered, "Let's go inside."

They walked across the deck, through sliding glass doors, and into the living room, lit only by one dim lamp.

"Oh, this is the most beautiful room I've—" Elizabeth began.

"You're beautiful, too, Liz," Bruce interrupted as he pulled her onto a large white couch and began kissing her again.

"Ummmm, Bruce," she murmured.

"You like this, don't you, Liz?" He let one hand slide lightly onto her breast, waiting to see if she would protest.

"That feels so good, Bruce." Elizabeth sighed and ran her fingers through his dark hair, then pulled him closer.

Elizabeth couldn't see his triumphant smile and didn't know he planned to gloat about his victory over the girl who had always snubbed him.

As he kissed her neck and held her close, Bruce urged, "Let's go upstairs. I'll show you what love is all about. Just the two of us, sweet Liz."

"No, Bruce. I can't—I shouldn't," she protested.

"Yes, Liz, yes," Bruce said. He caressed her shoulders, then lightly ran one hand down her thigh. "You want to say yes, I know you do."

Bruce got to his feet, took Elizabeth's hand

gently, and led her to the stairway. He was half afraid she would change her mind on the way to the second floor. Never had a conquest seemed so important to him.

"You're wonderful, Liz. Wonderful and sexy and beautiful," he said again and again between kisses as he guided her up the curved staircase.

Elizabeth kissed him back passionately.

Bruce reached the master bedroom, walked across the room, and placed Elizabeth gently on the king-size bed. She locked her arms around his neck, a dreamy smile on her lovely face. He pulled her hands away and kissed her hard on the lips, almost too hard, before he straightened.

"Don't go away. I just have to get the wine from downstairs, and I'll be right back." Then he was gone.

While Elizabeth was lying on the bed in the beach house, her mirror image, Jessica, was following the old bit of advice that says, "Don't get mad, get even."

Jessica had been interested in Bill Chase at one time. Something about his looks and style of living had intrigued her, but he had never paid any attention to her. One time she'd even gone so far as to ask him to a Sadie Hawkins Day party. He'd said very casually, "Sorry, can't make it." When it came to memory, an elephant's was fleeting compared to Jessica's—especially if it involved a guy who had once snubbed her.

Bill caught the girl he thought was Elizabeth in his arms at the end of the beach club dance and smiled down at her. He had never expected an evening like this. "Elizabeth" was acting as if she cared about him in the same way he cared about her. When he suggested going out on the beach for a walk, she could hardly get out of the room with him fast enough.

As Bill and Jessica strolled out of the beach club, Todd was standing outside on the long redwood deck on the ocean side. He hadn't gone to the dance but had walked down to the club just to watch the waves breaking against the shore. He needed to be alone. He could see only the couple's backs, but Todd knew Elizabeth well enough to recognize her satiny blond hair anywhere.

Bill had certainly wasted no time getting together with Elizabeth, he thought unhappily. He watched as they strolled down the beach out of sight.

"Bill," Jessica said softly, tilting her head back, "I'm so glad you asked me out tonight."

"Really, Liz?" He knew he had never been happier in his life.

"Really, Bill. I've always thought you were a wonderful guy." *And you never appreciated it*, Jessica told him silently.

Stopping on the moonlit beach, they looked

141

deep into one another's eyes. Bill put gentle hands on Jessica's shoulders, drawing her close enough for a kiss. She moved even closer, putting her arms around him and kissing him back.

"Oh, Liz, I can't keep it in any longer. I love you. I think I've always loved you!" Bill declared.

Jessica pulled back a little and smiled a secret, knowing smile. "No, Bill, you love my sister. I'm certain you do."

"No, Liz, no," he said, hugging her. "Jessica may be your sister, but I don't even like her."

"I think you do," Jessica insisted.

"It would be impossible," Bill said. "Let's not argue about something so crazy." He tucked her arm under his and walked on. "There's a spot down here where the moonlight looks like pure magic on the waves."

Jessica just smiled and let herself be led along.

Elizabeth lay on the large bed, overwhelmed with an unfamiliar sensation. Suddenly she was frightened. But she shouldn't be. This was what she wanted to do, wasn't it? Bruce, she thought, that was it. She knew she needed Bruce to make her feel good again, but he was gone.

"Bruce," she called. "Bruce!" He'd said something about going downstairs. Maybe she should do something about her hair and makeup before he got back, she thought.

She got up from the bed and was groping

through the darkness of the room for the door when she bumped against a chair. Desperately she tried to keep from falling, but her foot was tangled in a throw rug. She fell to the floor, slamming her head against a heavy wooden table.

Elizabeth lay on the floor stunned, strange lights and noises whirling through her head. She was in a dark room somewhere.

What is this place? she wondered. *How did I get here?*

She sat up, managed to get to her feet, and realized she was in her bedroom. She sat on the bed, shaking her head to clear it.

"Did I buy a bigger bed?" she mumbled.

She glanced around, trying to recognize the contours and shapes and shadows, and then she realized she was not on her own bed or in her own bedroom.

She was still in the hospital, she decided. But that wasn't right either.

Finally Elizabeth stood shakily and took tentative steps toward a dark square that must be the door. Beside it, her fingers touched something. A light switch. She pushed it up, and light flooded the room.

"Oh," she gasped, looking around. She'd never been in this room before and had no idea how she'd gotten there.

Then there came another sound. Footsteps. Somebody was coming up the stairs. The sound got louder. Someone was coming toward the room. Elizabeth shrank back, terrified of learning who it could be.

Suddenly, in the doorway stood a person she had never expected to see. "Bruce!" she gasped.

Bruce lounged arrogantly in the doorway, a bottle of wine in one hand, two glasses in the other.

"Miss me, baby?"

"What are you doing here?" she asked faintly.

"What?"

"Where am I? How did I get here?"

Bruce smiled. "Playing games, huh? Here. Have a slug of this and you'll be fine."

Bruce held out the bottle and glasses. He poured wine into them as Elizabeth watched in astonishment. Had she come here with Bruce Patman?

"How did I get here?"

Bruce leered at her. "You got lucky, Liz."

"I don't know what happened, but I want to go home," she said.

"Home? After you got me out here and teased me? Hey, Liz, come on."

"Why are you talking like that?" Elizabeth asked, feeling panic inside.

"I'm not in the mood for questions, Liz," he said, putting the wineglasses on a table and walking closer to her.

Elizabeth backed away, looking at him with a combination of revulsion and terror.

"You've been coming on to me all week. Don't deny it!" Bruce sneered.

"I haven't! I *couldn't*. And you haven't answered my questions. Where are we? Did you bring me here?"

"I didn't *bring* you here. You came willingly. And you know it's my folks' beach house."

Elizabeth looked around, cocking her ear for any other sound.

"Where are the other kids? Who else is here?"

"Listen, you little tease, get off it! You wanted to be alone. Don't give me this Little Miss Innocent routine."

Elizabeth sank down on the bed in despair and confusion. Tears sprang to her eyes. How could she have let such a thing happen? She looked at Bruce.

"You brought me here against my will somehow," she accused. "You know I don't like you."

Bruce's heart sank at the words and at the look he saw in Elizabeth's eyes. There was that old, steady contempt he used to see every time he looked at Elizabeth Wakefield.

"Not interested in fun and games anymore, huh? Or was that all an act? It's not very nice to set a guy up, Liz," he said menacingly.

Elizabeth knew she had to get out of there. She lurched toward the door, trying to get past him, but he blocked her way.

"Where are you going?" he asked angrily.

"Let me out of here!"

"Oh, no, you don't. You're going to give me what I want, what you promised."

"I didn't promise. I couldn't have! Get out of my way."

Bruce grabbed her and pulled her close. He tried to kiss her, but she turned her face away and pushed with all her strength against his shoulders, trying to free herself. Roughly he seized her wrists, and she was helpless.

"I've got real strong hands, Liz," he said. "From tennis, see? Now, you listen to me. You give me what I want, or I'll tell this whole thing all over school. You want that? What would all your friends think of you then?"

He forced her closer, and with one hand he held her head and kissed her again. Then suddenly he gave a cry of pain and let her go. "Ahhhhh! You bit me!" he wailed, holding his lower lip.

Elizabeth leaped past him to the door, then turned to glare back at him. Bruce Patman was whimpering and holding his lip, in no mood to cause any more trouble.

"I never really knew what a coward you were until now," she cried. "Is that what all your big love stories are about, Patman? Taking advantage of girls who either don't know what they're doing or are too drunk to care? I don't know anybody lower than you are at this minute. And, listen, you want to tell this story all over?

146

Go ahead! Because I've got one to tell, too, and you won't look very good in it. You're a coward, Bruce Patman!"

Elizabeth ran, finding her way down the stairs, through the front hall and out onto the porch. She kept running until she felt sand beneath her feet. It was wonderful to know who she was and where she was again. A brilliant moon sailed through the dark sky, and she wanted to yell, "Hi, there, you old moon!" She wanted to thank the stars for still shining. The sound of the surf crashing on the beach was a symphony.

The lights of the beach club shimmered ahead of her. She raced toward them like a homing pigeon. She'd find people there, but more important, she'd find a telephone.

Elizabeth took the wooden steps two at a time, almost tripping at the top, but strong arms saved her from falling. She looked up and her eyes met Todd's.

"Todd! Oh, Todd, I've never been so glad to see anybody in my entire life!" she said, collapsing against him.

Todd was, to say the least, startled.

"What—?"

"Todd, help me!" she implored.

Todd stepped back a little, his hands on her shoulders, and looked for a moment into Elizabeth's eyes. Those beautiful sea-colored eyes were the ones he knew, the tearstained face was the one he loved.

"It's you, Liz," he cried. "It's really you!" He pulled her into the warm safety of his arms.

Elizabeth shuddered and held on for dear life. "Oh, Todd, I don't understand what's happened."

"It's all right, Liz. Everything's all right." Todd held her closely, stroking her hair with a comforting hand. "You don't have anything to worry about now. You're safe, Liz. You're safe."

"I didn't know how I was going to get away from him. I don't know how he got me into that awful place."

"Don't worry about it. You haven't been yourself for so long." He looked into her eyes again anxiously. "You are back to being Elizabeth, aren't you?"

"Todd, of course. Who else would I be?"

"Never mind. There'll be time enough to talk about that later. But if Bill Chase did anything . . . I mean, he's supposed to be my friend. I can't tell you how jealous I was when I saw you on the beach with him."

"Who?"

"It's all right. I saw you with Bill. But that doesn't matter as long as you're back."

"But I wasn't with Bill Chase. It was Bruce Patman. How I could have spent a second with him is beyond me."

"But I saw you two on the beach together. If you were with Bruce, who's with Bill?"

148

They looked at each other, and the same name popped out.

"Jessica!"

Todd laughed with relief. "How do you like that? It was only Jessica."

Elizabeth shook her head, trying to straighten out her thoughts. Jessica with Bill Chase?

"What's the matter?" Todd asked.

"Bad news," Elizabeth said.

"You mean he's up to no good?"

Elizabeth shook her head sadly. "I'm afraid it's Jess who's up to no good. Bill Chase turned her down one time, and she's always sworn to get even with him if she ever got the chance."

"Well, it's probably nothing serious," Todd said. "I'm just so happy to have you back!" He grabbed her and held on, his powerful hands gripping her trembling body tightly against his. Elizabeth felt herself overflowing with love and appreciation for this strong, safe boy who held her with such passion.

"Todd," she breathed, and her mouth was on his in a deep, long kiss that she wished would last forever.

Bill and Jessica had reached that special sand dune he had mentioned, and now they stood in the moonlight, locked in each other's arms.

"Look at me and tell me again," Jessica told him.

"I love you."

"And not my sister?"

"No, never. I couldn't possibly love anyone but you."

"What's so special about me, Bill?"

"Your smile, your warmth, the sound of your voice, the touch of your lips, the feel of you in my arms. I've never been surer of anything in my life."

Jessica smiled. "Then you *do* love Jessica Wakefield, Bill, because that's who I am!"

Is Bill Chase caught in Jessica's trap? Find out in Sweet Valley High #8, HEARTBREAKER.

SWEET VALLEY HIGH

Bantam Books presents a Super

Surprise

Three Great Sweet Dreams Special Editions

Get to know characters who are just like you and your friends . . . share the fun and excitement, the heartache and love that make their lives special.

☐ 25884 MY SECRET LOVE #1 by
              Janet Quin-Harkin. $2.95

☐ 26168 A CHANGE OF HEART #2 by
              Susan Blake. $2.95

☐ 26292 SEARCHING FOR LOVE $2.95

You're going to love
ON OUR OWN®

Now starring in a brand-new SWEET DREAMS mini-series—Jill and Toni from *Ten Boy Summer* and *The Great Boy Chase*

Is there life after high school? Best friends Jill and Toni are about to find out—on their own.

Jill goes away to school and Toni stays home, but both soon learn that college isn't all fun and games. In their new adventures both must learn to handle new feelings about love and romance.

☐ 25723 #1 THE GRADUATES $2.50
☐ 25724 #2: THE TROUBLE WITH TONI $2.50
☐ 25937 #3: OUT OF LOVE $2.50
☐ 26186 #4: OLD FRIENDS, NEW FRIENDS $2.50
☐ 26034 #5: GROWING PAINS $2.50
☐ 26111 #6: BEST FRIENDS FOREVER $2.50

ON OUR OWN—The books that begin where SWEET DREAMS leaves off.

Prices and availability subject to change without notice.

Bantam Books, Inc., Dept. OO, 414 East Golf Road, Des Plaines, Ill. 60016

Please send me the books I have checked above. I am enclosing $_____ (please add $1.50 to cover postage and handling. Send check or money order—no cash or C.O.D.'s please).

Mr/Ms _____

Address _____

City/State _____ Zip _____

OO—4/87

Please allow four to six weeks for delivery. This offer expires 10/87.

Special Offer
Buy a Bantam Book
for only 50¢.

Now you can order the exciting books you've been wanting to read straight from Bantam's latest listing of hundreds of titles. *And* this special offer gives you the opportunity to purchase a Bantam book for only 50¢. Here's how:

By ordering any five books at the regular price per order, you can also choose any other single book listed (up to $4.95 value) for only 50¢. Some restrictions do apply, so for further details send for Bantam's listing of titles today.

Just send us your name and address and we'll send you Bantam Book's SHOP AT HOME CATALOG!